TELEPEN

80

D1144598

CPC UCW
LLYFRGELL
LIBRARY
ABERYSTWYTH

OC
STOCK

The Fruit
of
Thy Womb

Also by Herberto Sales

*THE WEREWOLF
AND OTHER TALES*

HERBERTO SALES

The Fruit
of
Thy Womb

Translated by Michael Fody, III
Foreword by Antonio Olinto
An Appreciation by Rebecca Catz

WYVERN 1982

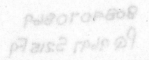

This translation first published in Great Britain by
Wyvern Publications Ltd
Bringsty, Worcester WR6 5UQ

© Herberto Sales 1982

ISBN 0 9507839 1 9 √ BRN

Printed in Great Britain

COLEG PRIFYSGOL CYMRU
THE UNIVERSITY COLLEGE OF WALES
ABERYSTWYTH

ACC No. 8084070869

CLASS No. PQ 9697 S215 F9

Contents

Foreword

In its recent upsurge in popularity, due mainly to the international success of the books of Gabriel Garcia Marquez, the South American novel has received fervent praise but perhaps has not been fully comprehended. The roots of this misapprehension probably lie in the fact that we all tend to accept easy generalizations about foreign nations and their people, and this in turn leads us to adopt preconceived ideas about their way of life and their achievements. In the North–South dialogue (or perhaps 'confrontation' would be a better word) it is customary for the Northern countries to regard the Southern countries as exotic. South America is a favourite target for this description. South American landscapes look exotic and therefore the inhabitants of the region must also be exotic. Of course the South American novel would also be as exotic, as exotic as the South American taste in food, clothing and politics.

To borrow the dichotomy used by Colin Wilson in one of his books, we could say that, according to this view, the North is *solar* while the South is *lunar*: the North is intellectual and scientific whereas the South is intuitive and magical.

However, it is known that there are many South Americas, just as there are many Europes, and the fact is that South American literature has experimented with many different styles, in the same way as the literature of other parts of the world. The three most famous contemporary South American writers of fiction—the Brazilian, Jorge Amado; the Argentinian, Jorge Luis Borges; and the Colombian, Gabriel Garcia Marquez—all show three different stylistic approaches to literature. Borges' style is the most European of the three. The strange pathos of some of his stories places him closer to Kafka than to his compatriots. Amado represents the *joie de vivre* of the Afro-Brazilian community of the Atlantic coast: he is the novelist of the common man of Bahia, of the epic times of the cocoa boom. Marquez reflects the tragic outlook of life on the Pacific coast: the beauty of his prose enhances the primitiveness of the social milieu he describes.

The Brazilian author, Herberto Sales—whose short-stories, *The Werewolf and Other Tales,* have already been published in the United Kingdom—cannot be framed into any preconception of the exotic South American author. It has already been noted that, in a country where the literature tends to the baroque, he is clear, neat, to-the-point, with a great economy of words and a realistic eye for detail.

Herberto Sales' latest novel, *The Fruit of Thy Womb*, shows him in all his reserve, in his quiet and unobtrusive style of telling a story. The novel is bluntly ironical, intensifying the incongruities of technocratic folly, and beneath the firm structure of the narrative there lies an element of genuine satire.

After mankind acquired the ability to split the atom, authors have been restlessly speculating on the extent of the danger to which human folly could take us. But, before the bomb, they were afraid of another and perhaps more immediate danger, a danger that is just around the next corner. The danger is that of a strong, technocratic dictatorship taking over all the countries of the Earth. George Orwell had his own way of showing this danger, and we have seen the technocrats of both the First World and the Second World sharpening their weapons for the kill. (In the Third World technocracy is still linked to the *lunar* or magical way of progress, although some Third World countries have done their best to emulate their models in the First World and the Second World.)

To Herberto Sales, in his new novel, technocracy is worse than plain dictatorship because technocracy can be hidden inside democratic institutions. He shows technocracy in a satiric style, but it is a satire which grants no mercy to the reader. Rather than encouraging the reader to smile or just wonder and ponder, his satire has an irritating tone which goes beyond the realm of well-behaved literature. To achieve the effect of shaking his reader, Herberto Sales structured his novel in three layers: one short, one long, one short. The first, *The Rabbits of the Island*, is a short fable less than four pages long. The second, *The Island of The Men*, carries the bulk of the story in a series of very detailed descriptions of all the measures taken by the technocrats to shape the life in society according to their plans. The institution of numerous abbreviations (an alphabetic list of which appears at the back of the book) to name the various departments and sub-departments, sectors and sub-sectors, is also depicted with tireless gusto by the narrator who, from time to time, intersperces some lyrical, usually very short, scenes, which thus enhance the aloof directness of the so-called perfect rules which are arrived at to bring about 'The Final Measure' solution to the overpopulation problem. (A curious side to this part of the novel is that the reader may find himself or herself in agreement with the technocrats in recognizing that the problem is a real problem that does, indeed, have to be solved.)

The third layer of the novel, *The Book of the Son*, is a short part. It is written in a biblical style, with numbered verses, in almost an entirely different language from the previous two parts. In this part, the spirit of birth, of Christmas, blots out the problems of the technocrats and Teodorico (the main character from the previous part of the book) is also pushed into the background in favour of new characters.

Herberto Sales, who writes without the anxiety of *seeking the phrase* and yet maintains his faithfulness to *le mot juste*, is a South American author who is worthy of an international audience.

ANTONIO OLINTO
London, 31 July 1982

Part I

The Rabbits of the Island

One

Poor little rabbits. There were a lot of rabbits on the Island: white ones, grey ones, black ones, vari-coloured ones. But who told them to multiply like that? They lived in burrows in the fields men had planted. Later, their burrows no longer sufficed. They spread over the fields like a billowing, velvety, patchwork quilt. (There were some yellow rabbits, too.) They began to strip the fields and gardens of their harvest.

Now, men had planted vegetables to eat.

It also happened that they ate rabbits, too: stewed ones, roasted ones, grilled ones. But, who told the rabbits to multiply like that? They propagated, procreated and reproduced at such a rate that soon man could not keep up with them no matter how many he tried to eat. On the other hand, the rabbits, being so numerous, were eating everything that man could plant.

Then, man realized that there were more rabbits on the Island than there were people. This was a serious problem for man: he couldn't let the rabbits eat while he starved. After all, the rabbits liked vegetables, but so did man. And his gardens were being seriously threatened by the rabbits. If things continued this way, man would soon be without his vegetables. (Most of the green was already gone from the fields, the vegetable green, that is.) One could not think of reducing the number of rabbits by eating them instead of vegetables because the rabbits outnumbered men twenty to one. Besides, man ate rabbit *with* vegetables since he had discovered that rabbit was even more savoury when accompanied by greens.

Then, one fine day, man began to worry that the rabbits, after eating up all the vegetables, would stage a mass invasion of the city, competing with man in his own stores and

U.C.W. ABERYSTWYTH LIBRARY

homes for the rest of his food.

The populace was in a panic: if the rabbits invaded the city, they would do away with man's other food supplies just as they had done with the vegetables.

Why, the situation might even be reversed and the rabbits, once they had nothing else, would turn to eating men. This would mean the end of the Island and, naturally, of man although it could eventually be the end of the rabbits, too.

Men must survive because they were more important than rabbits.

A solution had to be found.

One was.

After all, man always finds a way of solving his problems according to human dictates—not rodent needs. There were a lot of rabbits on the Island, right? They were a threat to man, right? Okay. One day, men flew over the Island's fields in helicopters and for one week bombarded all the places where rabbits congregated. Thousands and thousands of desperate rabbits fled to the beaches. But knowing their fear of water, a fear equal only to that of being bombed, not one of them dared enter the sea. And so they were bombed on the beaches as well until the last one of them was exterminated.

And that's how the rabbits were eradicated.

Then man returned to his peaceful cultivation of the fields since there were no more rabbits left to disturb him. Of course, he had to stop eating rabbits, but man didn't need them to survive. He had his flocks in fenced pastures and he had his granaries. And now he had regained his gardens, forever free from the plague of rabbits.

But it happened that man began to multiply almost as fast as the rabbits had. After a while, as the rabbits had threatened man's existence, so did man come to endanger his own survival. There were just too many men to eat.

It wasn't a question of vegetables any more.

To put it succinctly, there were too many people for the amount of food produced.

Man was faced with a dilemma: either the population stopped growing or they were going to starve to death.

Now, since no one wanted to starve, man immediately

sought a means to avoid this disagreeable disaster.

The governor of the Island (who was the governor of men) met with his cabinet, composed of technicians, to carefully study the problem from, naturally, all technical aspects.

One thing was certain: as long as men inhabited the Island, they wouldn't suffer the same fate as the rabbits. After all, a man was a man, and a rabbit was a rabbit.

What to do, then?

There was only one thing: create a department through which the government could exercise control of the Island's birthrate, prohibiting the same type of uncontrolled population growth in humans as had occurred with the rabbits.

Creating a department was the government's way of demonstrating that something was being done as it should be. Which meant that nothing was done until a department had been formed to deal with the problem.

At least that's how the technicians reasoned.

And following this line of thought, they recommended the formation of the Department of Population Regulation and Nuptial and Collateral Counselling. The problem was controlling the birthrate, wasn't it? Okay. The Department of Population Regulation and Nuptial and Collateral Counselling would take charge of it.

But the creation of a department necessitated the creation of a corresponding logo. After all, the symbol was as important as the department itself, as his advisors explained. 'The logo embodies the concentrated message, the specific communicative context associated with the immutable nature of said symbol.'

In other words, the Department of Population Regulation and Nuptial and Collateral Counselling had to have their emblem. That's why emblems had been invented.

The acronym was chosen: DEPREGNACC.

A simple communications problem. Without a doubt, it was much easier to say DEPREGNACC than Department of Population Regulation and Nuptial and Collateral Counselling. Not only easier to say, but to memorize, too. Thus, the first step in controlling the Island's birthrate had been taken.

5

Naturally, to create this department, the government had to pass a law by virtue of which said department could operate. No department could possibly exist without the prior passage of some law. The law which created DEPREGNACC was the Family Planning Law, which the government enforced to the letter since anything else would mean starvation for the Island's population. After all, a law was a law. Rabbits couldn't know anything of law, but man could.

Part II

The Island of Man

One

Every pregnant woman had to report to the hospital to be registered and examined. The examination was to determine how pregnant she was. Women more than three months pregnant would be exempt from certain requirements. They could return home to await the birth of their child. DEPREGNACC's officials had received express orders to spare these women the fate of the pregnant rabbits, indiscriminantly killed during the recent rodent extermination programme. The government wasn't interested in killing pregnant women. It was only concerned with what was in the women's best interests. Producing babies could not compromise the survival of the Island community.

As for women less than three months pregnant, they would have to abort the foetus. They were calm about it though, because as everyone knew, at this stage of pregnancy, abortion was not dangerous. Besides, the authorities would give them every necessary medical assistance. No one would die from an abortion. Not to mention the fact that it was going to be free, too.

For months long lines formed at the hospital doors. But in spite of the enormous efforts and dedication of the medical teams, the examination didn't proceed with the desired rapidity. Who told so many women to get pregnant anyway?

Due to the backlog of appointments (in addition to the medical examination there were the DEPREGNACC statistical forms to be filled out and this took time) the status of many women changed with respect to the law. With long delays, women who once were less than three months pregnant and thereby automatically consigned to the abortion category, passed the three month limit and received their parturition licence. Thus, many babies were born that weren't supposed to be. A stroke of luck—especially for

9

those first-time mothers who had been dreaming of cute little babies crying 'Ma-ma. Ma-ma.'

Meanwhile, women in their fifth or sixth month of pregnancy, after waiting in line for weeks and weeks (in many cases the wait was much less), had to be hurriedlly removed due to labour pains. If they had been registered and examined in time, they could have gone home to arrange things for the baby. They were polite, though, and didn't complain. After all, DEPREGNACC officials granted them priority status, and had in exceptional cases allowed them to go to the head of the line.

Teodorico the shoemaker, observing his neighbours pass by his door (he lived in his shop), commented: 'For two months now I've had to make lunch. My wife is in line by daybreak. I was never one for cooking, but I can make do. The problem is that she doesn't like the way I season the food. There's always too much salt, or too little. She's always complaining about the seasoning when I bring her lunchbox to the line. It's a good thing she makes the dinner, because at 5 pm the hospital closes its doors. I'm not bragging but my wife is a terrific cook.'

Estêvão, Pedro and many, many other husbands who lived in their shops or worked out of their homes were in the same boat as Teodorico: their wives in line and themselves in the kitchen. Although they erred in the seasoning, they at least had something to cook, and took a perplexed consolation in the fact that they weren't starving yet. So at noon, in groups, they took their wives' lunches to the hospital lines.

Signs advised the women: 'For your own protection, don't get out of the line. If you are thirsty, ask a guard for water. Don't waste time going to the drinking fountain. Bring your own glass from home.' (The guards in charge of supervising the lines had been instructed by DEPREGNACC to bring water to the women.) Other signs read: 'Eating in line is permitted, but don't litter. Remember that this is a city, not a pigsty. If you need to use the facilities, call a guard.' (The guards also had orders to conduct the women to the restrooms without forfeiting their place.)

The women themselves were the first to recognize that

everything was well organized. One had only to call a guard and say, 'I've got to go', and after first giving her a numbered control card, he would quickly guide her to the ladies' lounge. It's true that a line often formed in front of the bathroom, but it was shorter than the one in front of the hospital. And the guards could always bang on the door and shout, 'Hurry up! You're not at home. Get going!' And the women got going as best they could and gave up their places to others. After all, doing what one usually did in the bathroom took less time than the medical appointment. The important thing is that their place in line was saved. This was accomplished no doubt because DEPREGNACC's authorities maintained good order.

As for the rest, on the day of the implementation of the Family Planning Law, the Director of DEPREGNACC addressed the populace by radio and television and left no doubt as to how the law would work. Although it appeared that eating lunch at home would facilitate matters, in reality it would just complicate things. It would affect the dispersal of the line with evident prejudice to the functioning of the medical teams. It was a question of technique. Of organizational technique applied to streamlining the appointment procedure. The reasoning was clear, wasn't it? Time spent in walking to and from the hospital after eating at home, plus time spent in lunching (no matter how fast one tried to eat), all added up to an enormous delay in hospital appointments. These delays were not in the best interest of the women, much less in that of DEPREGNACC. No one wanted such delays because, in a choice between losing time and starving to death, naturally anyone would prefer the former to the latter. The quicker the women were seen, the quicker they would be freed from the lines and the quicker the population would be freed from the fear of hunger. And the Director concluded, 'It is absolutely indispensible that we recognize our human condition. We are not rabbits. And, not being rabbits, for the sake of our survival we cannot permit the women to multiply like the rabbits did.'

'That's true,' concluded Teodorico as he listened to the explanation profferred by DEPREGNACC's Director.

11

'That's true,' concluded Estêvão.
'That's true,' concluded all the others.
And the women agreed, 'That's true.'

Two

Yes, it was true: the women wasted a lot of time going home to eat. DEPREGNACC was right: for the sake of order and expediency, the women would eat in line—but no littering! Lunchbags should be taken home and there disposed of, but no throwing them in the streets. And since the hospital restrooms were dutifully stocked with toilet paper, there could be no excuse for throwing paper bags down the toilet.

But . . . let's see what happened to Teodorico before the creation of DEPREGNACC.

Since his marriage, Teodorico had never hired a cook. His wife did all the cooking. She liked to cook, had a talent for it, and took pride in her creations.

Two months after they married, she became pregnant. Teodorico was ecstatic. He called his two best friends, Estêvão, the tinker, and Pedro, the latheworker, and opened a bottle of wine to celebrate the occasion.

Estêvão had been through this once before: he had a son.

'A toast to the future kid,' he exclaimed, raising his glass. 'May he be healthy. Mine's as strong as a bull.'

'Having babies is fine,' said Pedro, who had five of his own, like the steps of a ladder, 'but it's hell to raise them, to feed and clothe them until they're grown and on their own. But people manage. That's what men and women were created for, ever since the Island was the Island. There's an old proverb which goes: "Be fruitful and multiply." Soneone once told it to me.'

Raising his glass he cried, 'A toast to the future heir!'

'And it's going to be a boy,' Teodorico quickly added, clinging to the certainty of an heir, however uncertain his inheritance might be.

'A son, yes. A strapping youth. And he'll have his father's name.'

13

He raised his glass. 'A toast to Teodorico Junior!'

By the second round, they had emptied the bottle.

The shoemaker's happiness lasted more than those two rounds. But not more than two weeks. Ten days after the celebration, the creation of DEPREGNACC was announced.

There were three newspapers on the Island: *The Techjournal*, *The Technocracy*, and *The Technocratic State*. These along with two radio stations and a television channel constituted SCAN (State Complex of Amalgamated News), created by the government to keep the people well-informed. if the Island had an administration and the people needed to be well-informed about Island affairs, who better than the government to give them the undistorted truth? The public shouldn't have to be exposed to mediocre news rebuttals, imagining that one thing had happened when it was exactly the opposite. SCAN had the advantage of being able to provide the people with exact information regarding all matters.

'In summation, for those who want to be well-informed there is nothing more disagreeable than hearing opposing viewpoints.' (Quote from the news technician's operating manual.) So in their desire to avoid conflicting news accounts, and considering the fact that when more information sources are available, the more susceptible a story is to differing accounts, SCAN declared itself to be the only news agency on the Island.

Teodorico picked up *The Techjournal* and almost choked to death when he read about the creation of DEPREGNACC.

It wasn't possible!

He ran to his wife.

'Babe, they've ruined us. You've got to get an abortion. You're going to have to get rid of Teodorico Junior. How could the government enact such a law?!'

'But . . .' stammered his wife.

'No buts about it. It's here in the paper.' Teodorico pointed to the DEPREGNACC article. 'Every woman on the Island who is less than three months pregnant has to get an abortion.'

14

'Maybe they'll change the law. Laws always change,' suggested his wife.

It was a way of consoling herself and her husband. It would mean that the authorities would have to do an aboutface, but it wouldn't be the first time that they had wanted one thing one day, and another thing the next.

They went to bed thinking about a possible reprieve. Nevertheless, the next day his wife got up early to go to the hospital lines since that's what DEPREGNACC's authorities had ordered. All things considered, it was always better to voluntarily attend government convocations than to suffer the embarrassment of being forcibly dragged there by guards, as the law warned.

In spite of what Teodorico's wife hoped the law didn't change, not on that day nor on the following ones. After two months in line, though, her situation did change: triumphantly, she became four months pregnant.

Teodorico, who in the past weeks had been apprehensively counting the minutes and hours, recounted the months with his wife since she had missed her period. It turned out that she really was in her fourth month. The two embraced, almost crying with joy.

'Saved! Now they can't make me get an abortion,' she said.

'Thank God,' he cried, utterly relieved.

And he opened another bottle of wine.

This time, however, he didn't sound the trumpets of joy. No calling Estêvão the tinker, or Pedro the latheworker, nor anyone else. A drunken friend could spill the beans and it could just as well be to the authorities as to a neighbour. At least that's what Teodorico thought, fearing the consequences of indiscretion.

DEPREGNACC's officials might view a celebration as a deliberate act of defiance directed against the new law. Besides, since its inauguration, the notion of parenthood had changed. According to the new law, fathering a child was somewhat irresponsible. And how could a responsible person like himself, in the company of friends around a bottle of wine, celebrate an irresponsible act? He thought it over, and the celebration seemed even riskier when he considered that he was really only a prospective father. If they wanted, he might not even get to be a real father. Who could guarantee that the DEPREGNACC authorities, in retaliation for his celebration, wouldn't dispute the couple's calculations with scientific arguments? One word from a doctor, and they could change the date of pregnancy on the examination card from four months to three. And there would be his wife, in the abortion line with Teodorico Junior!

Fearing such a catastrophe, Teodorico shut himself up in the house with his wife. In secret (a secret which remained between them) they opened a bottle of wine—just the two of them. Not being as fond of the bottle as she was of the pots and pans, she accompanied him in the toast only. (He drank the rest of the bottle alone.) Thus, behind closed doors, with a salute to the fortuitous entrance of the baby into its fourth month of gestation, they transformed their happiness into a kind of conjugal conspiracy. And as happens to conspirators involved in a covert act they found that risk contains an element of worrisome fascination.

The next day, the wife returned to the lines to continue the wait for her appointment. And Teodorico, although he made little progress in improving the seasoning in his cooking, found that his mood was much improved. It was with the happiest face in the world that he walked to the lines, every day, carrying his wife's lunchbox.

Three

While the abortion process was stepped up (insofar as possible), the Director of the Council of Integrated Technology (acronymed KIT), called a meeting of the assembly. The frightening rise in the granting of parturition licences necessitated new studies regarding the control of the birthrate. Things weren't going as planned.

In truth, the obligatory obstetrical examination would inevitably lead to a turnover in the rate of hospital appointments with a gradual levelling off of the abortion line. At least, that's what the technicians had hoped. Women who had escaped abortion the first time around would not be so lucky the second. They all would have to get one sooner or later. It was just a question of the turnover factor.

The present turnover rate, however, did entail lengthy delays incompatible with the government's urgent need to find an efficient solution to the problem. After all, the community's survival (now imperiled) couldn't be dependent on a rotating system of fertilizations followed by abortions.

At the new meeting of KIT, the General Co-ordinator addressed the technicians.

'The Director hopes that this meeting will produce the definitive solution to birth control.'

In view of the fact that births were directly linked to demography the floor was given over to a demographics specialist. The co-ordinator asked him to expound on the problem from his authoritative perspective.

The demographics expert began.

'While the act of propagation of the species does not preclude the male's collaboration, the woman must be viewed as the principle cause of the demographic increase since it is she who conceives. In demographic terms, the child represents the PF (Population Factor) for the community.

17

This means that a community increases in proportion to the growth rate of the PF, that is, the number of new births. Thus, if it is the woman who conceives the child, it is she who must take responsibility for the rise in the PF index, which is a corollary to the rise in the birth rate. Now as we all know, it is necessary to combat this rate which has reached epidemic proportions here on the Island. An epidemic presupposes the existence of some agent of transmission. In this case, the epidemic is an uncontrolled population explosion, and the agent of transmission is the child, as viewed in demographic terms of the Population Factor. And how does one combat an epidemic? Obviously by eradicating the disease carrier. As long as the carrier is permitted to exist, the epidemic will continue to spread. Thus if the woman conceives the child and the epidemic is caused by the proliferation of children, there is only one way to eradicate the spread of this disease: halt the uncontrolled birthrate.'

'That is exactly why mandatory abortion was instituted on the Island,' added another technician. 'All eligible women are submitting to abortion.'

'Abortion is not the answer except as a stop-gap measure,' continued the spokesman. 'You must realize that abortion is a function of attainability. That is, it is attainable only in certain cases, as when the women is three months pregnant or less. Birth control, requires a different methodology. It cannot be dealt with solely in a physical or biological framework subordinate to the conditions under which women will or will not abort. Getting women to realize that they have no reason to put themselves in this position to begin with must take precedence over the simple fact of abortion.'

'I believe that what my colleague is trying to say is simply that women must comprehend that they should not become mothers. Or to put it objectively, motherhood is a waste of time,' said a third expert.

'Yes, at least as far as it compromises the survival of the population,' continued the spokesman. 'As you can see, birth control is not only a demographical problem, in its conventional meaning of occupying physical space as a result

18

of uncontrolled population growth; it is also a social problem. Thus, it must be considered from a sociodemographic viewpoint, with its implications for populational status.'

'What do you mean by populational status?' asked the General Co-ordinator. 'Please define your terms objectively. Everything you say regarding population is of extreme interest to the Director.'

The demographics expert bowed slightly. 'Of course. When I say populational status, I am referring to the conditions of life and survival which any population experiences within a determined social status. Thus, the social status corresponds to populational status, in the global totality of sociodemographic status. When a population lacks adequate means of production, its sociodemographic structure will be seriously threatened. This is what is happening here on the Island. Due to the uncontrolled rise in birth statistics the populational status is in critical danger. And it will not be simply mandatory abortions which will restore the necessary social equilibrium. The Island's population must be gradually reduced by 50 per cent over the next 20 or 30 years, or the means of production will collapse. Since one can't apply to men the same solution applied to the rabbits, it falls to the government to adopt an energetic policy of . . .'

'Just a moment,' interrupted the General Co-ordinator. 'I would prefer you to use some other word. The use of the word "policy" is repugnant to the government. "Policy" applied to government acts or practices implies the existence of a political administration. And our government is not a political entity: it's technical. We live in a technocracy, where all rights are equal before Technology. This is why our politicians were done away with and replaced by you gentlemen. That is, government by specialists who will find technical solutions to the Island's problems. Perhaps it would be more correct to use the word "strategy".'

'I withdraw the term,' agreed the spokesman. 'The word "policy" occurred to me as spontaneously as, well, let's say an obscenity would. Please forgive its improper use in such serious circumstances. Without a doubt "strategy" is the better term. Therefore, as I was saying, along with the emergency plan of mandatory abortion, the government must adopt an efficient contraceptive strategy.'

'May I interject?' interjected a lexicography specialist.

'Of course.'

'I would like to remind the assembly that the term "policy" and its derivatives have already been modified for the new dictionary now in preparation, to be officially adopted throughout the Island. Three days ago, in the University quad, DECOWL (Department of Communications and Oral and Written Language) incinerated the last 18,252 copies of the old dictionary by which the institutions of learning and the organs of written and oral communication governed themselves. (On the basis of false and obsolete concepts, I might add.) The entry "policy" fell into this category.'

'I fear we digress,' cut in the General Co-ordinator. 'As I already stated, use of the term "policy" is repugnant to this government.'

'As it is to all the people,' added the lexicographer. 'That's why the word will be entered with its proper definition. That is: "A pernicious activity, detrimental to the welfare of the people, once practiced in the former branches of government by individuals who duped the people into believing they represented the public's interests when they really didn't." Although I recognize that this is not exactly germane to the subject, I want to take this opportunity to inform my colleagues that DECOWL has given top priority status to the publication of *The Dictionary of Technical Terminology*. The *Dictionary of Customary Usage of Spoken and Written Language* is still in the research stages in DECOWL's lexicographics laboratory. I might add that DECOWL is making every effort to reduce our present vocabulary to the absolute minimum, especially in the use of synonyms, in order to make audio-visual-graphic communication and linguistic expression more precise.'

The General Co-ordinator gestured impatiently, and turned to the specialist in demographic affairs.

'Please continue. You spoke of a contraceptive strategy.

What are your thoughts along this line?'

'At this time, I'd like to propose a plan,' answered the technician.

And without further digression (in the interests of continuity of exposition he asked that there be no more interruptions), the demographer expounded on the contraceptive strategy for precisely 58 minutes.

(Later on we'll hear just what this plan was.)

A sound technician operating a high-precision, electromagnetic recorder was taping the discourse (the meeting had been taped since its opening).

Finally, the specialist concluded.

'That is all I have to say on the matter.'

'Any advisors who are opposed to the plan, please stand,' said KIT's President.

Everyone remained solidly seated.

'The suggestions presented in the plan seem to be perfectly reasonable,' commented the General Co-ordinator. 'Nonetheless, the tape must first be submitted to the Director before proceeding further. The President cannot waste time reading something which hasn't been approved on tape first. That is the system. The President can't waste time. No one can.'

He then turned to KIT's President.

'I'll take the tape with me.'

He put it in a black briefcase bound with gold clasps. (He wasted almost a minute in getting it open because the clasps had a secret locking arrangement and a combination dial.)

He turned to the plan's author.

'I'm sure the Director will want to meet with you to clear up any details. At least that's my feeling.'

'We are entirely at his disposal,' added KIT's President. 'It is an honour to be a part of the Council of Integrated Technology, a consulting organ advising the government.'

'There is no doubt that you form one of the government's consulting bodies,' said the General Co-ordinator. 'But bearing in mind the positive results of this meeting, it's possible that the Director will only want to consult with the plan's author.'

21

He closed the briefcase.

'Naturally, the plan will still have to go to SUPERCAP (Superior Consultants Planning Division).'

KIT's President was perfectly aware of the role he played in the hierarchy of the government's diverse technical bodies, ranked according to their specific attributes of technical expertise and interfaced within the administrative context. Thus there were neither undisclosed nor overt rivalries between the specialists of KIT and SUPERCAP. On the contrary, the defined responsibilities of each combined to form a functioning harmonious whole.

Unperturbed, KIT's President declared, 'Since there are no further matters to be discussed, and bearing in mind that KIT has complied with its responsibilities, the meeting is adjourned.'

The General Co-ordinator picked up the briefcase containing the tape and left.

Four

The Director asked the General Co-ordinator to come in and close the office door. It was a large room, divided into two levels, with all the dramatic impact of a stage. On the first level was the furniture, flawlessly arranged: easy chairs, armchairs and a large, rectangular table with engraved panelling on the front and sides. On it, conventionally arranged like chessmen set up for a game, were desk accessories. On the wall behind the table, the Island's flag (fire engine red) hung down straight and even. A kind of long, lateral platform constituted the room's second level, with the back wall entirely covered by an illuminated map of the Island, mounted on five large plaques soldered together. Small flashing lights designating cities, towns and villages dotted the map; removable numbers indicated the population indexes for the various demarcated areas. All the lights were red—a sign that space was at a dangerous premium. But with the opening of the Contraceptive Campaign, the Director was sure that the colour of the lights would gradually change as the population levels decreased in the various sectors, until one day, the whole map would be green—the target colour showing the demographic equilibrium necessary to save the Island from starvation.

'Roll the tape immediately,' ordered the Director to the General Co-ordinator.

And sitting down he assumed an air of concentration, chin resting in his hand, eyes fixed on the maps' red lights.

The General Co-ordinator was a myopic little man who in the last two years had successively used wire-rimmed glasses, tortoise-shell glasses and finally contact lenses. While they changed his appearance somewhat, none of them managed to soften the metallic frigidity of his stare.

He walked over to the Director's private tape recorder

installed in a small metal table mounted on castors and put on the tape. A click was heard (a kind of metallic pinch) and then the silence of the room was filled with the meeting's technical parlance in which the Contraceptive Strategy was presented in great detail.

The Director continued to stare at the red lights of the map.

And while the electromagnetic tape spun from one reel to the other, he seemed to see the lights changing from bright red to red-orange and finally to a vibrant, brilliant green. At that instant, as though he wanted to retain his vision of the illusory, colourful metamorphosis, he brusquely turned away from the map.

The tape ended with the closing remarks of the specialist in demographic affairs: 'That's all I have to say regarding the matter.'

'Perfect,' commented the Director. 'I think our problem is solved.'

'What are your instructions?' asked the General Co-ordinator as he turned off the recorder.

'Leave the tape in the machine and call a meeting for today of SUPERCAP's technicians.'

'Do you think KIT will have to reconvene?'

'Absolutely. KIT's general assembly has already reviewed and approved the plan, so request only those technicians who are directly concerned with the problem. I want to meet with them informally before SUPERCAP's plan is implemented.'

The General Co-ordinator bowed slightly. 'That's what I thought you would want.'

Proud of his perspicacity, he smiled in the depths of his bureaucratic soul (or structure), secretly congratulating himself.

'I imagine that the author of the plan should also be present, don't you agree, Mr Director?' added the General Co-ordinator. 'It may be necessary to clear up any unforeseen details.'

'Yes, you're right,' agreed the Director. 'Invite SUPERCAP's sociopsychologist, the specialist in mass psychology, the sociodemographer . . .'

24

If you will permit me, Mr Director, I should remind you that the plan's author is a specialist in demographic affairs.'

'That's all right,' said the Director. 'I'd also like to hear the sociodemographer. Also, socialized medicine and the specialist for topical prevention and control. Set the time for 3.00 pm.'

The General Co-ordinator bowed and left, taking the briefcase with the gold clasps with him. But, naturally, he had been careful to take down the names of the specialists to be present at the meeting. Although he trusted his memory, he didn't want it exposed to the embarrassment of an unpardonable convocational oversight.

At 3.00 pm (on the dot), SUPERCAP's experts and the spokesman for the plan met in the Director's office.

The tape was replayed, and the demographer had the opportunity to listen to himself speak while SUPERCAP's experts heard his taped exposition. After 58 minutes (precisely), the General Co-ordinator quickly stopped the recorder.

'What do you think of the plan?' said the Director to the specialists.

'It is truly extraordinary,' answered the socio-psychologist. 'The plan will contribute to the formation of a new type of socioanalytic character on the Island.'

'There is no doubt that it is an eminently efficient plan,' said the specialist in mass psychology. 'From the viewpoint of mass response, it will promote a reformulation of the genital concept applied on a collective scale. Within a reasonable period, we will have established the basis for a new structure of the masses.'

'As an idea, it is excellent,' concluded the mass communications technician. 'The problem now is how to phrase it in communicative terms. Everything will depend on the message. That is, on the means of communicating the idea to the public. I am referring to the message as means: the means of motivating the people to accept the idea. I suggest that the plan be succinctly and clearly edited in order to validate its meaning and widen the message's impact.'

'I also feel that it's an extraordinary plan,' said the sociodemographer. 'I recognize that its implementation will lead to an extremely favourable modification in the community in terms of the dynamics of its individual and social norms of behaviour.'

'What seems to me to be of prime importance,' declared the spcialist in socialized medicine, 'is that birth control, in the terms proposed by the plan, does not involve any unnatural measures. Or, to be more clear: it does not impair any of the organism's operations. I am referring specifically to the organic function of sex, as corollary to the social whole. Actually, the plan should prevent conception without causing sexual frustration.'

'It seems to be perfectly feasible,' said the expert in topical prevention and control. 'I would prefer to hear if the plan's author has any additional details to add before I formulate any technical observations from a preventative viewpoint.'

The Director turned to KIT's technician.

'Do you have anything else to add?'

'No, sir,' he answered. 'Nothing else. Or rather, everything I had to say has been said and was heard on the tape. As author, though, I would like to express my thanks for the generous reception the plan has met with from SUPERCAP's technicians. I am at the disposition of the expert in topical prevention and control, should it prove necessary, to clarify any matters.'

'My observations will relate to any preventative measures required by the plan in its sector co-ordination phase,' clarified the preventions and control specialist. 'In the first place, since we have a plan, we should give it a name. What shall it be?'

The other technicians looked questioningly and somewhat startled at each other.

'Well . . .' finally ventured the author. 'As you gentlemen should have gathered from hearing the tape, the plan is based on a p . . .'

He was going to say 'policy', but, after a momentary pallor, he quickly corrected himself.

'. . . is based on a contraceptive strategy.'

Serenely he looked toward the Director.

The General Co-ordinator nodded his head in relieved confirmation.

'Exactly,' he said. 'The plan is based on a strategy.'

And he in turn looked (significantly) at the plan's author.

'In that case, considering that a contraceptive strategy is the goal of the plan, I think we can purely and simply call it Contraceptive Strategy,' added the mass communications specialist.

Everyone immediately approved the idea.

'I further suggest that it be abbreviated to CONSTAT,' continued the communications technician. 'It's a euphonic acronym integrating the fundamental syllabic entities of the plan's designation, based on the best techniques of logogram formation. I don't believe that another grouping of initials of equal communication impact could be found. It's not only mnemonic, but visual as well.'

Everyone immediately approved the acronym.

'Would you make a note of the plan's name and respective logo for the record?' said the Director to the General Co-ordinator.

He had no sooner done so when the specialist in topical prevention and control requested the floor.

'Now that the plan has a name, we must conceal it until the moment of implementation. Or better yet, until the moment its revelation is most opportune. It's a question of prevention. After all, if the plan embodies a strategy, it must involve strategic means of secrecy in its preparatory phases. In this sense, in addition to the logo, we must give it a code name. Exactly as is done with battles. A battle, as you gentlemen know, is a specific action whose success depends on the success of a series of parallel and convergent operations. Now, for all intents and purposes, CONSTAT (Contraceptive Strategy) is nothing less than a battle in which the government will engage to halt the population explosion. Although in this sense it will be a battle consisting of one operation only: the planned contraceptive operation. It is necessary, therefore, that a code name be created in order to conceal the operation's workings until the moment of assault.'

'And what name, or rather, codename do you propose?' asked the Director.

'Well, . . . it's always wise to choose a misleading code name for the operation,' answered the specialist in topical prevention and control.

And, after a pause, he said, 'It could be . . . let's see . . . Operation Violet.'

'Why "Operation Violet"?' asked the Director with interested curiosity.

'Simply because I remembered the violets in my garden. Just this morning my wife filled a vase with some.'

'Don't you think it's a little too romantic?'

'Yes, without a doubt. But that's why it fulfils all the requirements of a code name: it makes one think of something totally different from what is really being considered. After all, there is nothing less romantic nor more realistic than birth control as the Island's only means of salvation.'

'Perfect,' agreed the Director. 'Your argument is absolutely flawless.'

This was enough for CONSTAT to be henceforth called (codenamed) Operation Violet.

'Do you have anything further to add?' asked the Director, turning to regard the specialists with a look filled with the dynamic impetus of achievement.

Not hearing any other comments he turned to the General Co-ordinator.

'Present the plan to SUPERCAP at once.'

Five

Teodorico packed the lunch, left his assistant (the tinker Estêvão's teenage nephew) in charge of the store, went out and caught the bus to take lunch to his wife waiting in the hospital line.

Two days before, DEPREGNACC had proposed some modifications to the law. It wasn't that the law was going to change, at least, not in the way that Teodorico's wife—hoping for a reprieve—had imagined.

Let's see how the law would be perfected.

At first, only pregnant women were called for obstetrical examination and verification of abortion options, but later, DEPREGNACC's authorities decided to send KIT a proposal extending the requirement to all women capable of becoming pregnant. The only exceptions were to be prepubescent girls and women over 70—the age that DEPREGNACC had identified as being impossible for a woman to have a baby, even in highly unusual cases.

KIT met in extraordinary session. Photocopies of the proposal had been previously supplied for study to the specialists in attendance.

Opening the session, KIT's President said: 'As you gentlemen all know,' etc., etc. And he explained in brief words that they were meeting to consider DEPREGNACC's proposal. Without a doubt, it was a valid idea. But there was one problem to consider: KIT's previous suggestion, Operation Violet, was still under study by SUPERCAP. Since KIT had already proposed and forwarded one plan to the committee, KIT was in a rather delicate situation with regard to examining DEPREGNACC's proposal and later forwarding *that* to SUPERCAP. What would SUPERCAP say, after unexpectedly receiving a second proposal when the first was already a *fait accompli* in terms of Operation

Violet's framework. One must not forget that there was an operation in the works: Operation Violet.

'Given this, what do you propose?' asked a specialist of KIT's President.

'Purely and simply, I would propose shelving the idea, unless it undergoes such revisions as would be produced by an explicit regard for the refinement of the current birth control law. DEPREGNACC is facing serious difficulties in its work, difficulties impossible to overcome without adopting the methods defended in the proposal it deemed necessary to submit to KIT.'

'Yes, but in that case what do you propose?' insisted the specialist.

'I would propose a halt to forwarding the proposal to SUPERCAP until the details of Operation Violet's co-ordination have been concluded, unless DEPREGNACC, as it has done, insists that the recognized obstacles it now faces be overcome,' replied KIT's President.

'Then what is your proposal?' again insisted the specialist.

'I propose that we examine the proposal,' the President finally decided. 'The desirability of halting its submission to SUPERCAP doesn't prohibit us from examining it.'

At that point, putting in order the typed sheets he had brought with him and had been reading until that moment (in reality, zealous of final minutia, he had been re-reading them and had made some handwritten alterations during the session itself), the distributions specialist requested the floor.

Everyone turned in his direction.

And gathering his papers and the photocopy of the proposal into a stack foretelling of personal contributions to DEPREGNACC's proposed measures, he began to speak.

'The proposal offers a thematic nucleus of great importance to the contraceptive campaign. This—the thematic nucleus—would be enough to justify not only the approval of the plan, but also its immediate submission to SUPER-CAP without any inconvenience to Operation Violet. On the contrary, this thematic nucleus permits the expansion of a series of opportune suggestions which could only be of benefit to Operation Violet's framework. In reality, instead of clashing with any facet of KIT's proposal DEPREGNACC's plan actually complements it. Which is the same as saying that it complements Operation Violet. In highlighting the significance of its thematic nucleus, I would like to specifically refer to the idea, undoubtedly highly interesting, of dividing the women into categories, for purposes of their general assembly, with a view to obligatory obstetrical examinations. Naturally DEPREGNACC's proposal suffers from a lack of adequate technical structuring which, nonetheless, does not invalidate it as an idea, nor as a thematic springboard. In my capacity as distributions technician, I've taken the liberty of reformulating some of the items of the proposal in question, in the interests of technical organization.'

He paused and turned to KIT's President.

'If you would permit, I would like to elaborate on some of these matters.'

'This committee has the greatest curiosity in hearing your expert opinion,' answered the President.

'Thank you very much,' rejoined the technician.

He consulted his papers.

'As everyone knows, to improve the efficiency of the contraceptive campaign, DEPREGNACC has proposed dividing the Island's women into categories based on probable occurrence of pregnancy. Now, from a distributions viewpoint, dividing the women into categories presupposes their division into groups. I propose, therefore, that instead of dividing them into categories, they be divided into groups, each group to be based on a pre-determined category. Consequently, they will be divided into groups after an order of categories has been established. Which is the same as saying that they will have to be classified according to the category of each group. In short, there is no way to divide them into groups without first classifying them, just as there is no way to classify them without first establishing, for the diverse groups, their respective gradational standards by which the women, classified according to the characteristics of each group, will be sorted into their respective categories.'

'Would you permit me an observation?' asked another specialist.

'Of course.'

'I can't resist the temptation to interrupt my esteemed colleague to congratulate him on the objectivity and lucidity of his presentation of the problem.'

'Thank you,' said the speaker.

And he continued.

'In short, the problem is one of distributions technique, expressed in terms of definition of categories, based on criteria of previously established classifications by which the women will be sorted according to their group standard and, necessarily, divided into groups. Thus, a woman—or the group individual—will be integrated into her specific group and, at the same time, motivated to assume in relation to the group the same responsibilities which the group assumes in relation to her. These responsibilities have a common objective—that is: renouncing motherhood, in the various circumstances under which it could occur, as a means to the survival of not only the individual, but of the group and by extension of the whole Island community.'

(Applause. And throughout the assembly, amidst the applause, heads nodded in agreement. 'Very good! Very good!')

The distributions specialist interrupted his discourse for a moment. The incentive of applause was equal only to that of the attentive and curious silence which was gradually restored and he resumed his exposition as soon as he was able, speaking for another 45 minutes.

On and on he praised and defended the idea of grouping women according to DEPREGNACC's proposal.

The sections of his scheme under consideration were: (a) the groups, according to the nature of the group categories, and (b) group categories, according to their respective classifications. Finally, based on the categories established in his scheme, the women were divided into groups thus:

First Group—All women living in a state of admitted wedlock, whether by marriage or cohabitation. In the files,

32

civil status would be indicated by 'married' or 'co-habitating'. It was no longer a question of summoning pregnant women only—but all Island women, without discrimination. This must be understood. After all, the problem wasn't solely and simply one of pregnancy, subject to or exempt from abortion; it was a problem of conception prevention, instituting socioprogrammatic norms of community behaviour *vis-à-vis* sexual relations: no babies!

Continuing:

Couples who were married should so declare, presenting their marriage licence for the record. Unmarried couples should admit to a state of common-law wedlock as long as it was public knowledge as is characteristic of this type of union. It wouldn't matter if the woman were single or divorced. Just as a single woman (for whatever reason) might prefer living with a man over marrying him, so a divorcee had the same right to arrange for a companion and live with him as husband and wife instead of remarrying. In any case, a woman's freedom to form an alliance would be recognized. But women beware! In the interests of feminine-group surveys, no single or divorced woman could claim that status while at the same time openly living with a man. The obligatory notation on such files would be 'cohabitating'.

But, if such a woman (single or divorced), living in a state of public and acknowledged common-law marriage, should obtain a separation from her companion—how would that be noted on her file?

This problem, raised by one of the family planning specialists, was promptly dismissed by the speaker who had foreseen such developments in his notes.

He answered.

'Once the group classifications have been established, the authorities cannot take into consideration the hypotheses of failure of extramarital unions: only sociocommunal factors, or rather, the intrinsic, factual aspects of these unions should be considered.'

Although apparently satisfied with the explanation the family planning specialist persisted.

'Yes. But you must agree that separation can occur.'

'Absolutely,' responded the speaker. 'Nevertheless, in the case of a separation (divorce between married couples, or the break-up of an extramarital union), everything can be reduced to a simple change of status.'

'I see,' said an expert in organizational systems. 'For example, it means that in the case of separation by divorce, the couple will be classified as divorced, and will remain as such until they form a **new** relationship, correct?'

'Not exactly.'

'Not exactly?'

'Right. Not exactly.'

'I would like my esteemed colleague to clarify the matter,' rejoined the family planning specialist. 'At the beginning of your exposition you made it perfectly clear that the classifications would be 'married' and 'cohabitating'. You didn't mention 'divorced'.'

'Exactly.'

'Exactly?'

'Yes. And for one simple reason: divorced women don't necessarily constitute a group. Thus, they can't be classified under the first group—married or cohabitating—nor under any other grouping. Taking into consideration that their position, in the distributive structure, should be evaluated in terms of a subsidiary relationship to the first group, of which they will constitute a kind of reserve line, they—the divorcees—will actually be a subgroup. Thus, they will not be subject to the classifications of the first group but to a subclassification of that group. I believe that this provides the clarification requested by our esteemed colleague.'

The family planning technician nodded his head.

'Yes, without a doubt. Yes . . . I understand. I see that it is a problem of conjugal relationships, based on distributive data. Exactly. Exactly.'

The specialist in organizational systems assumed an intelligent expression.

'Yes, yes; I, too, understand. In other words, supposing a separation by divorce occurs, the civil status of the divorced couple will be not exactly classified, but subclassified.'

'Exactly,' confirmed the speaker with a solicitous air.

'They will be subclassified as "divorced", until a new alliance occurs. In the case of an extramarital union, they will be moved to the "cohabitating" classification, as they had been previously moved from the classification "married" to the subclassification of "cohabitating".'

'Then, you mean that the divorcee will serve a kind of term in the subclassification status which will then permit her to return to the classification status, right?' asked the organizational systems specialist.

'I wouldn't call it a "term", or at least, not categorically so,' answered the distributions expert. 'However, it seems impossible to ignore the fact that a subgroup classification does carry with it a connotation of interim stay. Nonetheless, with a new union, the divorcee will automatically return to her classified status, although under a different heading if the union occurs under extramarital conditions. Naturally, I am referring to the classification of "cohabitating". In the meantime, should a recidivous matrimonial union occur, the divorcee will simply be reinstated to her classification of "married" since it will be her second marriage.'

'And if there isn't a new union, that is, or a new extramarital, or marital . . . marital . . . just how was it that you classified a case of new union by marriage?'

'Recidivous matrimonial union.'

'Ah, yes . . . Recidivous matrimonial union. And should there be a new union,' he asked, 'which is neither extramarital nor recidivous matrimonial, how will the divorcee be classified in relation to the group?' insisted the organizational systems technician.

And with typical organizational preoccupation: 'After all, we must admit that she may reject the idea of a new union of one kind or another.'

'Your question is its own answer,' said the distributions expert. 'As long as the union, of whatever kind, remains unconsummated obviously the divorcee will remain in the subgroup category.'

'With your permission and that of your colleagues, would you permit me an observation?' asked the specialist in norms of socio-sexual behaviour, momentarily embarrassed. Well-versed in his field, he had thoroughly researched and documented his speciality in his dissertation *The totality of Sex or The Function of Sex in Societies' Fabric or On the Presence of Man and Woman in Society and Their Relationship After the Male-Female Conjugal Bond.*

(The book was sold out.)

'Of course,' said the speaker.

'I suppose,' said the author, 'that the divorcee's term in a subgroup does not negate the possibility of occasional sexual relationships, that is, sexual relations which are not necessarily dependent upon the types of union outlined in the classifications.'

'Obviously,' responded the distributions technician. 'We live in an advanced society which has broken with all structures repressing sexual liberty. The classification of women proposed in my plan, based on methods suggested by DEPREGNACC, is merely a means of statistical distributions control.'

'I believe it would be more appropriate to use the term ''conception control'',' interrupted the organizational systems expert.

'Conception control does not exclude the control of statistical distributions,' responded the speaker. 'Anyway, as I was saying, in an open society such as ours the plan to classify women will not interfere in any way with the sexual freedoms women have won. One has nothing to do with the other.'

'Bravo!' cried the expert in family planning. 'Nor would it be possible to conceive of sexual freedom replacing the family as a social institution. Within the family structure the married woman will continue to be faithful to her husband. For a married woman, sexual liberty exists only as far as it permits her to break the marriage contract in order to be with another man who exercises an attraction over her which her husband no longer can.'

'Whatever the case, one must admit that, in terms of sexual liberty, a married woman could give in to the temptation of an amorous adventure without necessarily having to break the conjugal contract,' mused the author of *The*

Totality of Sex or The Function of Sex in Societies' Fabric,
or On the Presence of Man and Woman in the Community
and Their Relationship After the Male-Female Conjugal
Bond. 'After all in the case of a lover, without previous
amorous experience, the married woman wouldn't be able to
fully evaluate the nature of the attraction that this man has
for her, as compared to her husband's possibly waning
charms.

'I protest!' exclaimed the family planning specialist. 'You
misinterpret the meaning of my argument. When I referred
to the inevitability of an attraction between an unmarried
man and a married woman, I did not do so with the intention
of promoting adultery; I was merely recognizing her right as
a human being not to be legally bound to a man she no
longer cares for. Actually, the law facilitates divorce in cases
where the affection which led to the celebration of the
marriage contract has cooled. Nonetheless, adultery . . .

The President of KIT interrupted the speaker by ringing an
electric bell.

'Please!' he cried, after the shrill ringing had achieved the
desired silence in the assemblage. 'We are getting away from
the question before us. We are here to examine additional
measures suggested for the contraceptive campaign and not
to meddle in matters of a private sexual nature. Let us be
aware of our role: we are a board of specialists, not a
subordinate censorship committee reviewing erotic-amorous
adventures.'

He turned to the distributions expert. 'Would you be so
kind as to resume your exposition?'

The specialist consulted his stack of typed pages and began
to speak.

'Mr President! The Second Group, that is, the next group,
will be composed of widows with the exception, naturally, of
those over 70 years of age. Strictly speaking, the widows
should be classified as a subgroup of the First Group, as the
divorcees were. But, in the case of widows, just as with
divorcees, there continues to exist the possibility of a new
union by a subsequent matrimonial bond. Or—to define
this new possible union using the strict terms of our

classifications—by a new marriage or by cohabitation. At the same time, while giving the widows the prerogatives of an independent distributive classification, or a status equal to that of group, without, nonetheless, denying the possibility of a new union, I would like, Mr President, to pay homage to the memory of one of the illustrous founders of the Technocracy, the Widow, of Matias M. M. McGregor, who with a dedicated sense of participation financed by her donations the installation of the Island's system of electronic computers in the ex-monks' monastery of the ex-brotherhood of ex-servants of ex-God.'

'Very well,' said KIT's President. 'The homage is appropriate, and it has, as it could not fail to have, this assembly's unrestricted approval. However, I would ask in these reminiscences that you not bring up old religious fanaticisms, and that you use proper terminology in referring to the building where the Island's system of electronic computers is installed, a system of which we are justifiably proud.'

'Of course,' said the specialist. 'If I didn't do so before, it was only because it seemed opportune to emphasize an important moment in our process of breaking with the structures of socio-religious repression. It is clear, therefore, that I was referring to the Central Institute of Technology housed, thanks to the Widow Matias M. M. McGregor's material assistance, in the architectural complex converted from the ex-monastery of that ex-religious order.'

And after consulting his stack of papers one more time he continued.

'The Third Group will consist of single women. When I use the term "single", I am referring to an independent sexual status characterized by noncommitment to any type of public union, either marital or extramarital. As we all know, prostitution was eliminated on the Island some years ago.'

'Just a moment!' interrupted the family planning specialist. 'I hope you're not trying to brand or classify our single women as ex-prostitutes.'

'I consider your comment to be impertinent,' protested the distributions specialist. 'Prostitution does not exist on the

38

Island. Thus, in establishing the characteristics of a determined group, I can't base my opinion on non-existent data. Since the institution of obligatory work for females . . .'

'One moment!' the family planning expert again interrupted. 'I hope that my esteemed colleague does not forget to emphasize in this respect the status of "professional", guaranteed by the Order of Mandatory Feminine Employment, which housewives now justifiably enjoy as co-maintenance household agents.

The distribution expert looked surprised.

'The Order of Mandatory Feminine Employment is totally outside the scope of the proposal to classify women. Besides, the proposal receives its consideration based on socio-conditioning data regarding gestation; it does not reflect a specific professional group viewpoint. If I mentioned mandatory feminine employment, (in response, I may add, to your first interruption,) it was not with the intention of dealing with its administrative function but merely to remind the assembly that since the Order's inauguration, no woman on the Island has had to make a living through prostitution.'

'But, what about the veto of the optional right of prostitution?'

The question was posed by a specialist in prevalent community optional norms who then moved from interruption to argumentation.

'The simple abolition of having to support one's self by prostitution would not be enough to eliminate prostitution, in view of its conventional acceptance as a profession, if it hadn't been accompanied by the veto of the optional right to prostitution. Just the opposite: in spite of the creation of the means by which an ex-hooker could earn her living in the normal job-market, there would always be the possibility of her continuing to be a prostitute. Therefore, it is important to remember that the elimination of prostitution was due not only to the institution of mandatory female employment, but, above all, to vetoing a woman's right to opt for prostitution whatever the circumstances. This veto, complementary to the proclamation of the Order of Mandatory Feminine Employment, was the deciding factor in the elimination of prostitution and consequently, the non-existence of prostitutes on the Island.

'Without a doubt, the veto was an important factor in the social recovery of the prostitute community, today entirely extinct, or socially recovered,' observed the specialist in sexual norms of behaviour. 'One must recognize, however, that a decisive contributing factor was the sexual liberty won by the individual-mass, in the process of breaking with the old, repressive socio-community structures.

'If you please, would you limit your discussion to the issue in question,' said KIT's President, zealous about maintaining good order, which was again threatened by the digressions which the speakers delighted in introducing. (At this rate, they would never reach a conclusion.) 'Since there are no more hookers on the Island, there's no sense wasting time discussing them.'

He gestured toward the speaker.

'Any other group to be considered?'

'Yes, Mr President. There is the Fourth Group, which is also the last. That is: the group composed of virgins. Now that this Board offers as factual data the sexual liberty won by the Island's female community, I'm afraid that the proposal regarding this group's composition might seem inadequate to meet the consociate norms which shape our social status. All of us are aware, naturally, that women are born virgins and fortunately, that they can remain so until they become adults. Thus, virgins would inevitably have to be considered in the distributive evaluation plan which I took the liberty of elaborating upon after DEPREGNACC's proposal.'

'Perfect!' cried KIT's President in a tone of emphatic approbation. 'The validity of your argument is unquestionable. That women are born virgins is inescapable. It is a biological inevitability. Besides, had the cult of virginity been eliminated from the Island's socio-communitive context, the eradication of this repressive and archaic cult would not lead necessarily to the elimination of virgins. Virgins may be insignificant, as they actually are in terms of the ethical-matrimonial conceptualization; but that

40

they exist cannot be denied. And existing, they cannot be omitted from a socio-classificatory scheme aimed at the general regimentation of the Island's women by way of their division into groups. Thus, there is nothing inadequate in your proposal regarding the composition of this fourth and last group. On the contrary, this group's inclusion only highlights your perfect adaptability to the proposal's theme.'

'Thank you,' said the speaker, as he picked up his typed sheets. 'Mr President, in my capacity as distribution specialist, it has been my duty to make the amendments to DEPREGNACC's proposal contained in these pages. Actually, the proposal is quite clear in its objectives. As I had the opportunity to point out at the start of my discourse, the proposal lacked only an adequate technical organization. I tried to provide this through an in-depth analysis of the proposal's motivational concepts, evaluating them not as isolated factors, but as elements integrated into a framework of global character, with a view to establishing a convergent operation.'

'Bravo!' applauded the organizational systems specialist. 'All convergent operations are derived from a framework of global character which determines in the search for established objectives the means of achieving them by means of converging operation.'

'Exactly,' rejoined the speaker. Your observation about the search for established objectives is well taken. Actually, where there is an established objective, there is necessarily a basic motive preceeding its establishment; and, considering that each objective is conditioned by the previous establishment of means to achieve it, this means that between the means of achievement and the objective itself, there exists the same antecedent relationship existing between the established objective and the basic motive by which it was established. Thus, DEPREGNACC's basic motive is the intensification of contraceptive reliability, to the extent that their objective is the division of women into categories. This presupposes, in distributive terms, the division of women into groups. Then, if DEPREGNACC follows the Board's conclusions regarding the proposal in question, I'm certain that this Board will take into consideration the alterations I have proposed, based on the establishment of methods which shape the feasibility of the proposal's motivational objective.'

The President looked at him with an air of unsatisfied curiosity.

'Yes . . . yes. You have established the methods which shape the feasibility of the proposal's objective. There is no doubt that you established them, giving the proposal the technical organization which it needed for the indispensable adjustment of its conceptual theories to reasoned, practical situations. Nonetheless, before putting your proposal to a vote, I would like you to clarify how desirable it would be to estimate the division of women into groups, and just what this desirability consists of.'

'Just a minute!' interrupted the specialist in statistics. 'If you will permit me, this matter has already been sufficiently clarified in DEPREGNACC's own proposal. It's a normative case of statistical desirability. That is: it is a question of statistically measuring a given fact with a view to establishing a conclusive relationship between the fact and its inferential statistics. After all, statistics are the measure of all things.'

The President nodded in the direction of the distributions expert who then responded.

'Mr President, the validity of my esteemed colleague's observation, anticipating my own answer, cannot be ignored. In fact, the proposal does involve a statistical dimension, which means that it should be considered in view of the degree of statistical advisability which will statistically measure the diverse groups into which the women will be divided during a statistical survey of the female population capable of pregnancy. After all, what does DEPREGNACC want? It hopes to extend comprehensively the obstetrical examination to all Island women except in those cases outlined where it would be obviously impossible. That is, except in the case of prepubescent girls and women over 70.'

'Right,' answered the President.

The speaker resumed.

42

Until now, the obstetrical examination has been operating as an emergency plan to control the birthrate by means of corroborating the viability of an abortion. Which is the same as saying that the plan is functioning not in terms of a global contraceptive strategy, but in terms of one particular fact: cases of declared pregnancy. Now, what does this mean? It means that contraceptive reliability, basic to the Island population's survival, contains the seeds of its own destruction in as much as the obstetrical examination, should it disprove the viability of abortion, leads inevitably to a licence to give birth. Thus, if in the actual context of contraception abortion does not preclude the possibility of birth, it becomes more important to halt a pregnant woman's chances of avoiding abortion than to control pregnancy dependent on abortion. In a word, we must control conception.'

A sudden round of applause, indicating enthusiastic acceptance of the idea, briefly interrupted the distributions expert.

'Thank you, thank you, thank you,' he said, as he repeatedly nodded his head to all points of the assembly.

He waited until silence had been restored.

'Mr President! The Government must prepare itself to unleash, via Operation Violet, a massive contraceptive campaign based on the mandatory use of the pill. The pill obviously is the most reliable means of preventing pregnancy at this time when, as I pointed out before, it is imperative to prohibit pregnancy, since by prohibiting pregnancy, we will also prohibit a rise in the population index which is of serious concern to us all. And it is exactly in this area, Mr President, as I had the opportunity of pointing out in my initial remarks, that DEPREGNACC's proposal compliments Operation Violet. Besides, by forwarding its proposal for this Board's approval, DEPREGNACC did nothing more than attempt to adjust its goals to Operation Violet, recognizing that mere control of the birthrate would be inadequate as a control of (or a simple correction to) the Island's population explosion. Thus, Mr President, although to verify the possibility of an abortion in cases of declared

43

pregnancy the obstetrical examination should continue to be mandatory, it behooves us to extend it comprehensively, as DEPREGNACC suggests, to all Island women, whatever their category or group, in the interests of verifying or rather catching a pregnancy in its earliest stages, before even the woman herself suspects it. The medical teams naturally have the technical precision. As for the rest, the division of women into groups will create psychological conditions favourable to the initiation of an all-inclusive, obstetrical examination since it will contribute to the formation of competitive contraceptive teams of females, based on their very distributive categories.'

'Excellent!' said the specialist in organizational systems.

And he prolonged the applause with his own comments.

'You were very fortunate to express the comprehensive obstetrical examination in terms of the formation of female competitive contraceptive teams, although certain groups of women present, in relation to other groups, advantages which, strictly speaking, place them in a supracompetitive category. The single woman, for example, has a natural contraceptive supremacy over a married woman, although it is possible for her to become pregnant in the course of a casual sexual liaison. In any case, one must recognize that the establishment of a contraceptive competition between the various women's divisions will lead to a healthy, intergroup contraceptive emulation which will be of great interest to the global contraceptive campaign.'

'I feel obliged to correct one point of your analysis,' replied the distributions specialist. 'With the adoption of the comprehensive obstetrical examination, soon there will be no risk of a single woman accidentally becoming pregnant through—to use your words—a casual sexual liaison, simply because from now on, no woman will be exposed to the risk of becoming pregnant, no matter what the nature of the circumstances of her sexual liaison. After all, the comprehensive obstetrical examination's goal is to establish a preparatory process to prevent conception. And how will it do this? It will prevent pregnancy exactly as DEPREGNACC outlined in its timely proposal. That is, by the contraceptive equalization of the diverse groups constituting the Island's female population, resorting to abortion in those confirmed cases of pregnancy. In other words, the comprehensive obstetrical examination will establish a zero conception rate for the Island after which effective conditions will finally be created for the mandatory and systematic use of the pill as a means to prevent pregnancy, independent of the examination. Which is the same as saying that the comprehensive obstetrical examinination will be gradually phased out as the pill reaches a level of comprehensive use, permitting us to finally dispense with the examination.'

'Would you permit me an observation?' asked the specialist in fiscal administration and economic and financial provisions.

The observation was permitted.

'Of prime importance is the anticipatory factor of administrative placement of the comprehensive obstetrical examination since it involves, in its bidimensional economic-financial effects, *duration* and *extinction*. That is, with the exception of continual maintenance, it leads to a processing of budget factors destined to produce decisive results regarding the attainment of its programmed objectives in a perfect blending of opportune and economic factors. Actually, looking objectively at a reduction in consumer areas as a function of the application of corrective measures to the population explosion, the programme will last only that amount of time necessary to achieve its objective. Which means that it operates as a function of an investment programme which, directly linked to the time required to achieve its goals, will produce a rise in the population's economic levels as it eliminates cost expenditures in controlling the population explosion. In a word, if its tenure involves expenses, during its lifetime the programme will also produce an economy superior to the amount of expenditures involved in its duration. Thus, the factor of extinction is an administrative fact of great importance to the economic-financial processing of the proposal or, more specifically, of the obstetrical examination.'

'The observations which you just made are of great value in terms of the proposal's total impact,' said the distributions expert. 'Actually, in analysing it from the angle of your technical speciality, you have projected the extinction factor onto compatibility and contingency levels regarding prime advantages and secondary effects, technically characterizing it as a basic element of support to the execution of the programme contained in the proposal.'

'As far as that goes, there is no doubt,' interrupted the family planning specialist. 'I should add that everything seems to be well thought out. Only I don't understand why the obstetrical examination should be extended to include virgins. After all, virginity excludes the possibility of conception.'

'I remind my colleague that the obstetrical examination is 'If it's comprehensive, there can be no exceptions.'

'And prepubescent girls? and women over 70? asked the family planning specialist.

'I believe that's a sophist's argument,' countered another. 'The examples you cite cannot be regarded as examples. Obviously they are not examples of exceptions in the contraceptive context, but rather, concrete cases of the impossibility of pregnancy which is a totally different thing.'

'In any case, I insist upon registering my unease regarding the necessity of extending the obstetrical examination to virgins, although the comprehensive nature of the examination may rest upon this point,' said the family planning specialist. 'Considering that the family is an associative institution with a social value recognized by the technocracy, in support of my position I might remind one of the natural embarrassment which a virgin would experience being submitted to this type of examination, which would leave her open to her family's absurd and uncomfortable suspicions. I would prefer, however, to pose the problem in strictly rational terms: if virginity excludes the verification of pregnancy at any stage, why should DEPREGNACC want virgins to be included in the obstetrical examination? In short, of what use is this examination to virgins?'

'Of what use!?' cried the organizational systems technician. 'To my way of thinking, my esteemed colleague's unease is simply due to a problem of nomenclature. That is, if the obstetrical examination implies a state of pregnancy, then, naturally, it would be inappropriate for virgins, since if one is a virgin, there can be no conception. This, however, does not invalidate the need to examine virgins. Rather than them having an obstetrical examination, they will have—let's say—a gynecological examination. A simple problem of nomenclature. However it may be, considering that the loss of one's virginity may lead to conception, the utility of an examination for virgins is obvious: it will serve to verify if they are really virgins as they claim. This is, without a doubt, very important to the organization of contraceptive services, viewed in terms of the system. After all, the examination of women does follow a general system of verification.'

'I think it is ridiculous for you gentlemen to be worried about someone's virginity when women on the Island enjoy as a matter of law and fact the rights of sexual liberty,' added the author of the treatise *The Totality of Sex or On the Function of Sex in Societies' Fabric, or On the Presence of Man and Woman in Society and Their Relationship After the Male-Female Conjugal Bond*.

KIT's President once again rang the electronic bell.

'Please! Everything that needed to be said regarding sexual liberty has already been said. Therefore, I consider the reopening of this issue to be inopportune as it will only serve to prolong our work.'

He turned to the distributions specialist.

'You have the floor.'

'Thank you, Mr President,' he said, promptly retaking it.

He began in a tone of apologetic deliberation.

'There is no way to deny, Mr President, that sexual freedom, as already defined in our session, has just be re-examined at a very opportune moment, in view of the fact that an examination for virgins is actually a function of this liberty. As I stressed earlier, the comprehensive obstetrical examination aims to establish a zero conception rate on the Island, after which it will be possible to prevent pregnancy through the mandatory and systematic use of the pill. Thus, Mr President, virgins will also be required to use the pill as an antipregnancy measure against whatever circumstances the loss of virginity may occur. After all, in a regime of sexual freedom, the less conventional one's idea of a virgin is, the easier it is to lose one's virginity in the context of the individual's sexual behaviour *vis à vis* society. Which means that the incidence of loss of virginity in a sexually liberated society, will be more frequent if less importance is placed on virginity itself. Surely, our esteemed colleague in family planning must be aware of this. Therefore, as our organizational systems expert fortuitously pointed out, while not obstetrical but gynecological for virgins, the verification of virginity through examination will have in its apparent uselessness, the objective of placing virgins under contraceptive protection, in case they lose their virginity. Which means that virgins are naturally situated in the contraceptive equalization rank via the comprehensive obstetrical examination, with a view to the mandatory use of the pill, which will soon be established for all women capable of pregnancy according to their various distributive categories and to the type of sexual union existing in function of each particular group. Therefore, and I especially direct my attention to my esteemed colleage in family planning, the family institution will not be compromised nor affected by the fact of a virgin losing her virginity since the loss of such outside the sphere of matrimony does not constitute an impediment to her marriage with whomever and whenever she may please. Accordingly, if loss of virginity does not make a woman unsuitable for marriage, then in the sexually liberated regime the institution of the family is virtually invulnerable since a virgin, after the loss of her virginity, benefits as much from the regime of sexual liberation as from the institution of marriage. But we are all well aware of this as is everyone else on the Island. Then, what is in question here is not the exclusion of the possibility of marriage due to a loss of virginity from an extramarital affair, but rather that the loss of virginity in such circumstances could lead to pregnancy. Therefore, the examination of virgins is required as a natural consequence of the measures DEPREGNACC hopes to institute to place women under antipregnancy protection, including virgins who, classified in their proper group through verification of virginity, will be obligated to use the pill since virginity does not prohibit casual sexual affairs, in the global scheme of the sexual relations of the diverse groups into which women have been divided, from relation by marriage to that of casual relations.'

'Perfect!' added the organizational systems specialist. 'In summation, it is a question of organization. If the comprehensive obstetrical examination is to be instituted as such, there can be no exception. Either it's comprehensive or it isn't. Furthermore, the examination of virgins is expressed in terms of perfect appropriateness to the group total, since the girls will constitute a group. Nor could one understand how virgins, constituting a group, could be exempt from an examination whose total antipregnancy effects, in the interests of controlling the evils of the Island's population explosion, necessarily depend on its indiscriminate, all-inclusive application.'

'Neither foolish, family affections, nor a virgin's silly prudery, nor any simple-minded stupidity that smacks of the old, false morality will stop us from carrying out the comprehensive obstetrical examination. What matters, Mr President, what matters, my friends, is the Island, the survival of the Island's population, the starvation which threatens her, and that danger which can only be avoided by adopting this truly life-saving measure: the effective establishment of a completely foolproof contraceptive programme.'

His last words were met with a long round of applause. And while it lasted, all the family planning specialist could do was to raise one finger over his head and keep it there until silence was restored and the president granted him the floor, stoically claimed by his silent, vertical gesture.

'I want it to be perfectly clear, Mr President, that I am not against any measure leading to the establishment of a foolproof contraceptive programme on the Island,' he began. 'My only interest is to safeguard, within the contraceptive context, the institution of the family which will be included in one form or another as a function of planning criteria approved by the technocracy. Although in view of the reasons proferred I now recognize the plausibility of an examination

49

for virgins, it is my duty to call to the attention of this Board a subordinate facet of the problem: the systematic prohibition of offspring, in the case of a normative couple, does not invalidate the need for family planning. It will endure as a function of the necessities of budget and salary standards established by law as conditionary norms to the effectuation of marriage. The conceptual rethinking of the family, proceeding from the establishment of contraceptive controls, will create, at best, a new type of family which nonetheless will still be a family. That is: the family of two, or husband/wife to use its binomial expression. Then this new family, of necessity, will utilize the family planning service in so far as the new planned type of family assures the survival of the family as an institution in its socio-technocratic significance. That is, the family, not as an abstract entity based on mutual, abstract feelings of affection, but as an association realistically planned according to the economic means clearly at its disposal, and organized as such to maintain a level of viable associative security.'

'Of course, of course,' said KIT's President. 'It is a pleasure to see how you supported your contraceptive programme as a method of controlling the population explosion while, at the same time, making important contributions to bringing the problem into global focus, analysing it from your technical specialty's specific viewpoint.'

He turned to the distributions specialist.

'Your clarification of several points which were obscure to me was lucid and brilliant. And, having done so at my request, I would like to offer you my personal thanks. Nonetheless, before we put it to a vote, I would like to know if you have anything further to add.'

'Strictly speaking, Mr President, I wouldn't have anything further to say,' answered the distributions expert. 'But let my last words stress the fact that once DEPREGNACC's recommended measures are adopted, the use of the pill will be freed from the tutelage of an individual option and raised to the level of global utilization destined to promote the adjustment of generalized, contraceptive interests. It will no

50

longer be a question of whether or not to use the pill according to the whims of a certain person or groups of persons as has happened in the past. Actually, considering that an interest exists in function of an intentional behaviour in so far as that intentionality of behaviour exists as a function of producing a future state of affairs on an individual and social level—it behooves us to ask, is there, or is there not, a general concern for contraception on the Island? Of course there is. And it has as its determining cause the population explosion. And thus it was in the name of this general contraceptive concern that I appealed to this Board's superior understanding to approve all the measures in DEPREGNACC's proposal which I had the honour of explaining in technical terminology.'

Applause. Applause. Applause.

And, with that, the proposal was unanimously approved. Now, all that was left was to forward it to SUPERCAP for their consideration, via the usual channels for review of material not expressly solicited from KIT by the Director, via the General Co-ordinator, or, in some cases, via SUPERCAP itself.

This was done. On that very day, with the help of four typists certified by SICS (Situational Control Service) and three SNOWIN editors specialized in summarizing texts, KIT's secretary prepared for the president's consideration the proposal's dossier containing the elements stipulated for the presentation of the review of material of that nature. (That is, review of material not expressly solicited from KIT by the Director, etc., etc., as was the case with DEPREGNACC's proposal, elaborated on and ratified by KIT.) The dossier consisted of the following items or elements of textual-auditory elaboration: the general minutes of the session, the synopsis of the minutes of the session, the exposition, the agenda of the tape's text, and finally, the tape itself.

From his glass cubicle, while he was preparing to rerun the tape as many times as the summarizers considered necessary to compile the agenda's text, the tape operator saw KIT's experts leave the floor one by one. From behind the glass, in

51

the silence created by the disconnected microphones, they resembled an automated parade of dolls. Nonetheless, there was an unmistakable sign of life on their faces: the look of superior tranquility, flaunted in the certainty that all that they as specialists had advocated, or as experts had supported, was as simple in its execution as its proposition might appear complicated to the layman.

Six

Yes, Teodorico, just where was it that we left him? Ah, there he is, on the bus with his wife's lunchbox. He was lucky enough to get a seat. He's got the lunchbox cuddled in his lap in happy, concentrated zeal. He paid for one fare only since he's alone: at least that's what everyone thinks. A small, invisible passenger is accompanying him: Teodorico Junior, doubly conceived—in his mother's womb and in his father's head. In any case, children don't have to pay the fare. Now the lunch is cuddled in his lap, now it isn't. In its place is Teodorico Junior. The father seated, the child in his lap. The bus rolls on and on, halts at one stop and another, picks up (or lets off) passengers, continues on and on and on, with trees and streets passing across the silver screen of panoramic windows. One thing only did not pass: Teodorico's idea of fatherhood, his obsession. The sway of the bus created a rocking lullabye jingle in his head: 'Sleep, sleep, my little one.' Suddenly, the last stop brings him back to reality, with the last passengers moving to get off while the bus slowly, gently, draws up to the curb. Teodorico gets up. It's the end of his itinerant dream. He has arrived at Hospital Square, where the hospital is. Outside, he sees the line of women. He gets off the bus with the bundle, which is again a lunchbox. Anxious, he lets his eyes run over the line, to see if he can find his wife. She should be around there with her companions of the line, methodically arranged in the square under the orderly glance of the guards. The long, long line stretches around the plaza where four streets meet: S–18, S–5, S–14 and S–10. Urban spokes of which Hospital Square is the hub. No streets named after people.

'To make it known that a street is a street, it is enough to so indicate with a symbol; to distinguish among them, one adds to the generic symbol a conventional element of differentiation: the number assigned to each according to the urban planning blueprint.'

The specialists in urban nomenclature had decided this, and, because of its tight visual-communicative intuitiveness, they had adopted the initial of the word 'street'. Perpetuating the name of a specific person on a street sign, under the pretext of paying homage to him, was a typical manifestation of the cult of individualism, which the technocracy had abolished. (The technocratic society tends basically towards the suppression of individualism, substituting the collective body for the individual, in its social totality of the masses—item from the Technocratic Platform.) After all, an address (necessarily involving a street designation) implied a strict, practical use. It was a means by which one could be found or find someone else. The specialists in urban nomenclature had made this perfectly clear in their counsel concerning visual-mnemonic methods of intercommunicative orientation for pedestrians and vehicles. The advice was based on an urban assessment survey of the Island, carried out by a team of engineers from TechCen (Technological Centre). Yes, yes: if an address was the means by which one person located another, that did not justify the fact that said person, in order to arrive at his destination, was obliged to read a street sign with the name of a third person who had nothing to do with the other two. Besides, as had happened during times of extreme individualism, if certain persons resolved to honour another by naming a street after him, the rest of the population wasn't consulted regarding this honour. Why, then, must they forever be compelled to repeat in an address the name of a totally unknown individual; No, no, no, no. No streets with names of individuals. No old honorary plaques which, invading the streets, squares and avenues, had made urban raids on the alleys and by-ways in order to perpetuate the names of people on every corner. As was said, the criterion of names was definitely abolished.

'In a regime which eliminates the cult of individualism, the personalization of street names via the use of an urban nomenclature of ostentatious, individualistic connotations,

54

cannot be tolerated.' (Opinion of one of the specialists in urban nomenclature.)

'A negative conclusion leads to a negative experience. Thus, if the criterion of personalizing street names, or of streets with names of persons, is a negative experience, the conclusion one must draw from this experience is a negative one, in so far as the criterion which ordered and produced this experience is negative. And what must one do to correct a negative experience? Obviously, one must make use of its very negativity as a basis for a positive reformulation of the criterion which made it negative, substituting the opposite criterion which will be as positive as its opposite was negative. Which is to say that if the criterion of personalizing street names resulted in a negative experience, there is only one way by which it can lead to a positive experience invalidating the prior negative one: eliminate the names of people on street signs, adopting a criterion which will lead to the depersonalization of streets via the use of a system of impersonal symbols by which the streets will be known.' (Opinion of another urban nomenclature specialist.)

And, being interested in the complete implementation of the programme to eliminate the cult of individualism, of which the personalization of street signs was but one of the most typical (and pernicious) examples, they all agreed that there was but one truly efficient way to depersonalize the streets without compromising the methods of urban orientation: substitute numbers for the old names. The solution lay in impersonal numeration. And as one specialist pointed out, the more simple its implementation, the more desirable the solution's impersonal numeration was.

Implemented immediately, the programme was extended not only to streets with names of people, but also to those which, following popular tradition, had curious or picturesque designations linked to their origins. For example, Chestnut Tree Hill became S-23, although the S for 'street', used generically, might, in this case, lead to possible erroneous interpretations. After all, certain systematic souls, chained to the conventions of urban geometry, might think S stood for 'slope'. But alleys, lanes, roads and avenues were naturally exempt from this type of confusion, being urban thoroughfares not exposed to the subtlety of synonyms such as hill/slope, which led to the coincidence of S. In short, they were all streets, and each received its S (black on a butter-yellow background), followed by its respective number (ivory, outlined with a brilliant green border) on a large, square sign (80 cm x 80 cm) designed by DEVICOM (Department of Visual Communication), according to a system of joint optical centres. The technician for the assessment of addresses, after finishing, also pointed out that the new criterion of urban nomenclature represented a strong subliminal stimulus to a liking for mathematics, of undeniable benefit to the people. And attributing an additional leisure factor to numeration, he pointed out that any citizen, while waiting at a bus stop or on a corner for a friend, could amuse himself by mentally adding the street number to that of the adjacent buildings. One had to admit that this would help pass the time, freeing one from the tedium of an unfortuitously delayed arrival.

The only exception was for plazas, which continued to be so designated for purposes of demarcation of areas on the urban blueprint, where they would appear as glades amidst the forest of S's. The old public squares would also be in this category, but, in the interests of adopting a generic designation, as a counterpoint to the generic designation for a street, they would be considered as plazas. However, (as must happen) the personal names which they had previously flaunted would be eliminated, as they would for the plazas. Contrary to the case of streets, the plazas would not be designated by numbers nor by abbreviations. No one considered reducing them to a simple P, in view of the fact that they had received an urban emphasis by linking their names to bureaux, departments institutions or official entities which functioned in buildings situated therein. Thus, Baron of Cordelio Plaza became TechCen Plaza (Technological Centre) after, naturally, the baron's statue was demolished. Once the cult of individualism had been abolished, it would have been inconceivable to leave a marble baron sitting on a bronze chair in the middle of a plaza. Due to the law, and to some chiseling, the other statues were condemned to unappealable demolition, wherever and whatever they were—bust, monument, equestrian statue, or pedestal. In short: once the process of implementing the new urban nomenclature had been concluded (rapidly), the plazas were now duly depersonalized: the aforementioned TechCen Plaza, DEPREGNACC Plaza, DECOWL Plaza, KIT Plaza, SUPERCAP Plaza, etc., etc., a world of logos and domains where a few exceptions stood out—Palace Plaza (where the Director lived), Technocracy Plaza, Communications Plaza, Hospital Plaza, Plaza of the . . .

No, no, no.

Let's stay in Hospital Plaza where we left Teodorico, Island resident of S-821, B (for block) 23, H (for house) 18, SN (Sector North).

CENTRAF (Central Traffic) had blocked all entrances to the plaza, rerouting traffic to other streets during the schedule of hospital visits. With this the authorities hoped to demonstrate their zeal in preserving the integrity of the line, permitting it to keep its perfect formation as it slowly wound its way forward. The women would not be bothered by any passing vehicle which could force them to step out of line or which might run over one of them. And, proud of the organization of their services, CENTRAF was confident that the women would show their gratitude for this exceptional means of protection taken in their favour, assuring them during their long schedule and in their condition of pedestrian, exclusive use of an extensive urban sector, to the detriment of the customary flow of traffic. No one had any reason to complain, right?

But, what about the bus carrying Teodorico to the plaza? Well, there is always an exception that proves the rule, in the everyday world of rules and exceptions. If the rule was to block the plaza to vehicles, the exception was the bus that made the hospital its last stop. It drove, therefore, on the wrong side of the street, opposite the line which was in itself an exception—granted only during the hospital visit schedule. As for the rest, whether because of its specific objective of examining the women, or because of the

57

circumstantial presence of relatives bringing lunches, this gathering led to a constant flow of people to and from Hospital Plaza, and the authorities agreed to allow the visits, not by foot, but—as an exception—by bus.

Teodorico was walking. Popcorn vendors passed with their carts, acting in complementary fashion to the line by easing the tedium of a long wait with their cheerful, toasted kernels. A specialist in mass economy planning, consulted by DEPREGNACC, restricted the vendor's access to the line, vetoing the presence of other ambulatory vendors in the square. The motive: if on the Island there was a discrepancy between the production of food and the alarming growth of the population, then it was unjustifiable that the women, on whom the consumer equilibrium depended by reducing the birthrate, should be the first to set a bad example of domestic budgetary irresponsibility, stuffing themselves with candy, caramels, and ice cream. The ordinance received the whole-hearted approval of the specialist in mass psychology who judiciously concluded that popcorn vendors were enough to give 'local colour' to the scene. All in all, it was decided that no woman could buy more than two bags of popcorn, which was a means of assuring that they could eat candy and snacks. And to save them the trouble of having to get out of line to throw the wrappers in the urban trash receptacles, the vendors had to arm themselves with sacks to collect the papers. The sound advice of keeping the plaza clean was thus preserved, since everyone was to remember that they were in a plaza and not a pigpen.

And Teodorico was walking.

Due to his daily attendance at the line, many of the faces had become so familiar that as he scanned them in attentive search of his wife's, he felt irresistibly compelled to offer greetings which, for the same reason, were returned, since his noontime presence was no less familiar to the women. In spite of the lack of names and introductions a singular intimacy among strangers, born of that frequent encounter of familiar faces, had been established and nurtured along the length of that numerous and aligned pregnancy.

Their chats were lively, people talking without knowing to whom they were speaking; the long wait predisposed them to an uneasy necessity of saying or hearing anything which would help them kill time by one means or another. And, due to the effort of this reciprocal casual communication, there grew up among them an involuntary sort of solidarity, born of mutual care and courtesy.

Here are some excerpts from their conversations:

'Naturally. Aren't you tired?'

'No . . .'

'But you've been here in line for more than two hours.'

'You, too.'

'Yes. But I'm not as far along as you. I'm only in my fourth month.'

'I'm in my fifth.'

'So? You should rest a little. The boy who rents the benches should be along soon. You ought to rent one. A seat always helps.'

'Oh, thank you. I'm not saying that I don't like to sit down. But, perhaps there are no more benches left. As soon as he arrives, he rents them all.'

Other excerpts:

'Please, sit down.'

'And you?'

'I've rested enough. I can stand for a while.'

'That wouldn't be right. You rented this bench.'

'It doesn't matter. I've been sitting for quite some time, and I can loan it to you. Don't stand on ceremony.'

'Oh, thank you.'

More excerpts:

'That boy who rents the benches has sure been a help.'

'I'll say! But he should bring more of them. What he brings is never enough.'

'Don't you want to sit down?'

'Oh, no. Don't bother.'

'It's no bother. It's a small bench but there's room enough for two. Sit down, sit down.'

'Oh, thank you. What a relief! This little seat came just in time.'

Like the muffled hum of a beehive, the line buzzed in animated conversation. If silence was golden, it wasn't seducing anyone there with its promise of wealth. Talk, talk, talk. After all, conversation was the only means by which they could stand (amusing themselves) the sacrifice of such a prolonged, drawn-out wait. Oh, how sweet it was to be able to chat, to talk with someone! Thank goodness they hadn't prohibited talking—since no one had taken advantage of the opportunity to slander the technocratically-composed authorities. Speaking badly of the authorities was prohibited because the authorities, working day and night for the Island, offered no cause to be insulted. Besides, there were many other things to talk about in line, and those same authorities, represented by the presence of the guards, condescendingly stimulated conversation.

'You can talk. Talk all you you want,' said the guards.

And everyone talked, talked, talked since there was always something good to talk about, which helped to pass the time in line. One need only choose subject. For example: popcorn. For example: the benches.

'Look there: your wife's being seen,' said one of the women to Teodorico as she saw him pass by with the lunchbox, anxiously looking for his wife.

He stopped short, experiencing an incredible joy. She was being seen! He couldn't believe that after three months in line, the day of the examination had finally arrived. And then, in anxious haste to see for himself, mentally adding up the months in line with those where she had skipped her period, he turned his eyes towards the hospital door with the fervour of one grasping at a last hope. Without a word, he ran to station himself on the sidewalk where he remained in immobile curiosity, stoically enduring the tense passage of time as though, instead of blood, his heart were pumping the trembling secret of his own anxieties. And totally oblivious to his surroundings, concentrating only on the examination's outcome, he remained there for an hour which lasted an eternity. Finally he saw his wife appear at the hospital door. He tried to call her, but, stifled by his anguish, his voice refused to work; and if his anguish hindered his voice, it also hampered his steps, bringing him to the ground like a statue of himself: a statue (if there had still been statues) of a man with a lunchbox in his hand, agonizing between the dream and the decree: between the desire to be a father and the fear that his wife no longer carried the child which he had fathered during the uneasy times of the mandatory abortion law. On impulse, as though breaking the links of an invisible chain, he raised the lunchbox up in the air over the heads of a confused group of people and gestured at his wife. In the relief of that gesture, perhaps grotesque, but in which there was true suffering and a desire to be seen at any cost, he managed to catch her attention. Seeing the lunchbox waving in the air, she answered it with a gesture of her own, waving a piece of paper with a smile of triumph and relief.

It was the signed birth licence.

For the first time in his adult life and since he had confronted life as a man, Teodorico discovered that he still knew how to cry. How silly! A man crying amidst all those people . . . His wife came up and tenderly led him over to a corner.

'What's this, dear? Everything turned out all right.'

'But, that's why I'm crying,' he answered, sobbing onto her shoulder.

Suddenly, conquering his emotion but not his curiosity, he dried his eyes with the sleeve of his coat and asked to see the paper. He wanted to see it, to read it because, assailed by a sudden and insidious doubt, he was afraid that there might still be the possibility of some trick—who knows? She gave him the paper. Greedy for the official truth, with his eyes still damp, he first read DEPREGNACC's official letter-head; then, the title: Voucher of Birth Licence. Finally, type-written, his wife's name (her full name) with the following summary notations: The bearer is authorized to carry her pregnancy to term, confirmed on this date. (And there was the date.) The current voucher is valid until the day of birth, after which the bearer, under penalty of law, is required to return this licence to DEPREGNACC. In case of loss or damage, the bearer may obtain a second voucher, the original control copy of which will remain with the authorities. A more or less illegible signature followed, in the curious fashion of official signatures produced by the tedium and the fatigue of an eternal signing of name.

Teodorico gave a sigh of relief. There was no more doubt. Teodorico Junior had been duly authorized to see the light of day. He took his wife's arm and the two got on the bus. They whispered together until they arrived home in mutual and jubilant planning for diapers, jumpsuits and wool booties.

Seven

The Contraceptive Strategy Plan, alias Operation Violet—
since the development of the plan was occurring under the
utmost secrecy, disguised with the misleading codename
recommended by the technician in topical prevention and
control, under the influence of his preventitive instincts—the
Plan (no, no, no), Operation Violet was well under way when
suddenly the complete dossier of DEPREGNACC's proposed measures arrived at SUPERCAP, duly ratified by
KIT who had given it the necessary technical organization which we already know about. Thus SUPERCAP's
specialists found out about it after we did, which is certainly
a privilege for those following this story—you and I. But it's
better not to get involved in these complications. Let's let
them follow their own course. If SUPERCAP's technicians
kept quiet about their plan, let us keep quiet about our
privilege. After all, we don't live on the Island, nor are we
technicians. Let's limit ourselves to seeing what SUPER-
CAP's specialists did when they found out about what we
knew before they did, thanks to the order of the chapters of
this book.

Then what did SUPERCAP's specialists do when they had
said folder in hand?

Well, first they tried to read it and evaluate its short,
medium and long term effects. And thus hierarchically considered, as far as terms can be prioritized like chronological
facts, the consequences gave favourable results in its analytic
evaluation. (This was the conclusion one of SUPERCAP's
technicians drew from the analysis of the dossier's material.)

'This means,' he added, 'that the consequences are
favourable. Thus, if advantages are evident from the
analysis of the consequences, the proposal to divide the
women in groups is useful.

Yes, it was, without a doubt, a beautiful and opportune idea. SUPERCAP's technicians (meeting in secret session) approved it without hesitation. Actually, they did vacillate on one point: deciding whether Operation Violet should take place before the women were grouped, or if their categorization should be integrated with Operation Violet.

'In my opinion, they're complementary since they imply the notion of totality,' said one specialist.

'They're complementary, but at the same time, mutually exclusive,' said another.

'What is complementary cannot be exclusive,' said a third.

But the second responded.

'It's a question of placement. One thing can be complementary to another through a process of convergent actions without these actions losing their exclusivity, by virtue of existing as independent facts. Operation Violet, as an aggregate of facts, is a whole, as the either. It was ready to go except for its official approval. Great!

Shortly thereafter, in a perfect blending of luminous controls and ceremonious actions, the outside red light which along with the help of four armed guards barred access by strangers to SUPERCAP's sessions, was turned off. In its place, a green one went on, the door opened, and the guards snapped to attention as the specialists filed out in grave silence, carrying their analysis of DEPREGNACC's proposal to the Director.

He had been waiting for no less since, after hearing the tape, he was aware of the proposal. He retained a favourable impression not only of DEPREGNACC's idea but also of KIT's technical organization of it. So favourable that he was disposed to approve it—as long as it was accompanied by SUPERCAP's assessment and that assessment recommended its approval. After all, grouping of women, in its aggregation of facts, is a whole. Therefore they should be mutually exclusive as two wholes in themselves. In other words, Operation Violet's implementation is independent of the categorization of women, although both plans share, as two wholes, an interrelated objective. Thus, if SUPERCAP approves the division of women into groups, let them be divided immediately according to a plan which, operating as an independent whole, must, as such, precede Operation Violet, and not be a part of it.

Well, in view of such convincing arguments, they overcame their doubts and SUPERCAP's technicians finally arrived at a general consensus: the division of women would be put into effect independently of Operation Violet which for its part was still in the planning stages, while the categorization of women was already complete. It was dependent neither on Operation Violet nor on any additional planning, there was a bureaucratic technique involved here, couched in technical bureaucratic terms, which the Director observed with strict, technocratic discipline—never to approve any proposal that did not bear SUPERCAP's seal of approval. Which it did have.

After reading it, the Director said, 'Perfect. There is no doubt but that the division of women should precede Operation Violet and not be a part of it.'

Once he read the recommendation, it was approved.

In half an hour SUPERCAP had prepared the decree and signed it immediately. On the same day, transmitted via the Island's communications networks which together constituted SCAN (State Complex of Amalgamated News), the edict became law.

Teodorico, thrilled with the birth licence his wife had finally obtained, didn't turn on the radio that day (he didn't have a TV), being occupied with making plans for the arrival of Teodorico Junior. He learned about the decree from the newspaper he had bought that night from the stand next to his office. He couldn't have missed it because the newsboy was continually shouting the headlines.

'Extra! Extra! New law for women!'

In startled curiosity, Teodorico grabbed the paper and read the edict.

'Thank goodness it's not what I thought.'

'What did you think it was?' asked his wife as she tried to read over his shoulder.

'Who knows; I thought it might be some law countermanding the previous one.'

And with a conceited air of relief, he summarized the decree for his wife.

'It's dumb. They're going to divide women into groups. But the law's the law. Get our marriage licence and go register us tomorrow with DEPREGNACC.'

'DEPREGNACC? Again?'

'No, not there exactly. They're going to set up some movable registration centres according to residential zones. The decree explains it all. They'll be no problem. You show the marriage licence and you get your file card certifying that you're married. Every group has a category, get it? Married, single, cohabitating. It's a life-long categorization. But, what's important is that the categorization won't interfere with the birth of our son.'

Reassured, his wife smiled happily but, at the same time, her eyes filled with tears. She began to sob softly, head down, as though ashamed of herself, of the weakness implicit in that sudden crying into which was mixed the remains of an unfounded fear and a rapid overflowing of thankful joy: the new law wouldn't stop her from becoming a mother. Her child would be born!

Hearing her sobs from behind, Teodorico threw the newspaper into a corner and got up, and curious, he tenderly embraced his wife.

'What's this, honey? Are you crying?'

Enveloped in mutual tenderness, without being able to find words for one another, they embraced lovingly in the emotional and silent certainty that sooner or later they would be three.[1]

---

[1] It's possible that neither their sentiments nor their mathematics were original. Let's forgive their arithmetic and the sentiments which led them to it. Whatever else, a couple given permission to procreate was closer to originality than to the routine or the ordinary on the Island.

Eight

Movable registration booths, used for the feminine group survey: in some cases, they used emergency medical services vehicles; in others, since there weren't enough vehicles to go around, they set up canvas tents which, scattered throughout the neighbourhoods, gave a lively, cheerful bazaar-like atmosphere to the scene. While they were shorter, new lines did form in front of the booths, but they moved rapidly since the people were seen according to blocks or 'residential conglomerates', to use the technical terminology of the decree.

Teodorico's wife went to the corner booth, presented her marriage licence, and received her married status card which the clerk (a man wearing a brown cap with DEPREGNACC's emblem pinned over the visor) stamped and signed. After all, where there are clerks, there are stamps, and a permit is always more of a permit if it carries a stamp. The second copy of the permit was placed on the second copy pile which a second clerk bundled into stacks fastened with rubber bands for later delivery to DEPREGNACC's archives. Perfect control. The computer would take care of the rest, computing the computable with the rapidity and infallibility of which no human mind is capable since the human brain invented the computer for no other reason than to demonstrate with humility and, at the same time, pride, that the computer is superior to the human mind.

Actually, as Teodorico had foreseen, there were no problems. Everything was quick and easy. Between going to the line and standing in it until reaching the counter where the man in the brown cap stamped her permit, his wife spent no more than 30 minutes. What a difference from the hospital appointment where she had spent three months in line! All in all, filling out a survey card at a booth was much less work than trying to find out in a hospital, with the aseptic and complex use of scientific instruments, if a woman was or was not in condition to abort, if she had to get rid of the foetus or continue carrying it until the day in which instead of a foetus, a brand new baby would be born. But when comparing the speed of attendance at the registration booths with the sluggishness of the hospital line, it was also necessary to consider that the lentitude of one line explained the rapidity of the other in so far as all pregnant Island women descended en masse on the hospital while at the booths, independent of their state of pregnancy, there only appeared housewives living in the urban area assigned to each kiosk. This advantage, from which his wife benefited at the booth after having passed through the hospital line, did not escape Teodorico's prediction of ease of certification. By her own experience in getting the voucher of birth licence and the group survey card, his wife was able to verify that the hospital line was as slow as the booth was rapid. So much the better! Happily she left the booth and returned home, card in her purse. Along the way she stopped at an ice cream parlour for a cone which, while it cooled her throat, did nothing to cool her joyful ardour.

While sucking on the snow cone she met one of her neighbours.

'Have you been to the booth yet?' asked Teodorico's wife.

'Yes, and I got my card already,' answered the other, momentarily putting down the straw (plastic) which she was using to sip the juice.

'The card is here in my purse,' she said, before returning to her cone. 'Wait a minute while I show you. Drat! Where did it go?'

'Don't tell me you lost it already.'

'No, no, no, no. I put it here somewhere. It's just that my purse is so full of stuff. Just a minute. Ah, there! Here it is.'

'But, yours is green? Mine is blue . . .'

'Right,' explained the woman. 'Each group has a different coloured card. To make it easier, understand? By the colour you can tell right away which group you belong to.'

'Clever! I didn't pay any attention to it. Besides, it was my husband who read the edict and he didn't tell me anything about any colour-coded cards.'

'He didn't need to. The clerk in the booth distributes the cards according to the colour assigned to each group. It's just like a game. For example, when I arrived there, he asked me if I was married, single or cohabitating, and when I said cohabitating, he gave me the green card.'

'Yes. More or less the same thing happened to me. Only when I said "married", he asked me for my marriage licence, examined the seal, and then gave me a blue card. I didn't even notice if there were cards of other colours. I thought all of them were blue.'

'It would have been funny if they were! Can't you imagine the confusion it would cause? If they divided us into groups, they had to give each group a different colour, or else how could they know which group we belong to? They're very organized.'

At that moment a neighbour of theirs passed by the ice cream parlour—a neighbour who was not only a neighbour, but a friend as well—something which doesn't always happen between neighbours, nor between acquaintances. The friendship, nurtured by proximity, prompted an interested and cordial curiosity in the two as soon as they saw the third woman walk down the sidewalk.

'Going back home already?' asked the second woman.

'Yes,' responded the third, entering the ice cream parlour.

The two invited her to sit down, but she, fanning herself with her card, politely refused the invitation; she was in a hurry and needed to return home right away.

'Wait a minute, then, and we'll go together,' said the second woman.

Hurriedly, she picked up the straw and in a short, slurping second, drank the remains of her fruit snow cone.

Teodorico's wife, between sipping the last of her drink and casting a curious glance at the card with which her neighbour was negligently fanning herself, remarked, 'You've got a yellow card.'

'It's the card for singles,' clarified the other in a tone of ironic indifference. 'While I'm single, this will be my colour.'

Without interrupting their conversation, they went outside and started home.

'And your boyfriend, when do you two plan to get married?' asked Teodorico's wife.

'When he makes enough money,' answered the other. 'For now he's not making the salary required by DEPREGNACC for a man to get married. If it were up to me, we would already be living together. He, however, wants to wait till we get married. Besides, thinking it over, why should we complicate our lives by living together, right? After all, when we want to get together, we go to his room and that's all there is to it. He has his freedom and I have mine. Marriage will happen when it happens.'

'As far as I'm concerned, it doesn't make a bit of difference one way or the other,' added the second woman. 'I'm happy living together and I'm not going to worry over a piece of paper like a marriage certificate. Paper for paper, I've got my card now. Anyway, even before DEPREGNACC's law went into effect, my boyfriend and I were living together. And together we'll continue because he doesn't make enough money, either, to get married.'

'Well, if the law had come out before our marriage, Teodorico and I wouldn't be married now either,' said the shoemaker's wife. 'Teodorico, poor thing, with the pittance he makes at the office, is miles away from making what the law requires in order to marry these days. When we got married, things were different: people married whenever and however they could.'

'Oh, come on! Getting married!' sneered the woman who lived with her boyfriend. 'The important thing was that people—single, married or living together—could have all the kids they wanted. Now, everything is different. No woman is mistress of her womb anymore. The boss of our wombs is DEPREGNACC.'

With brusque, nostalgic despair, mixed with the painful emotion of thwarted dreams and hopelessness regarding the future, she continued.

70

'Ah, those days will never return . . . Now, for a woman to have a child, she must depend on DEPREGNACC. DEPREGNACC is the one who decides if we can have a baby or not. Everything's changed on the Island now.'

They had arrived at their houses, next door to each other, almost at the end of the street. The conversation ended there with goodbyes, each woman returning to domestic chores interrupted by the formality of having to register; free of that duty, the women were now prisoners of their respective classifications. Yes, they were prisoners, now, a fact which seemed even more real to them after the conversation they had just had—and which they suddenly and acutely felt. It was no longer a question of simple social distinctions which they had ignored before anyway; it meant nothing that Teodorico's wife was married, one neighbour living with a man, and another, after having gone through several men before soothing her embittered romances with her current lover (a textile worker), was living the negligent freedom of a single's life, stimulated by overt and covert meetings in his room. Now—and the three felt this keenly—it was no longer the same. If their social situation had never before separated them—and not having kept them apart up to now, it had permitted them to enjoy the freedom of a communal social relationship, free from the old prejudices of by-gone days— the cards would divide them as members of differing groups. From then on, they would no longer be able to attend future meetings called under the law, nor stand in the same lines, nor seek aid together from the official bureaucratic windows offering various services which people inevitably submitted to during their routine contacts with official entities—since there was always some requirement between the people and the official agencies which could only be fulfilled with forms and stamps so that people could benefit in one form or another from the official entities. Ah, no longer would they be able to stroll along together thus occupied, conversing as friends and neighbours as they usually did while waiting to be seen. Now, each one would have to go her own way, ignoring proximity and friendship. What was important— and the three suddenly realized this—was the group each one

71

was to be a part of, and the perception that each belonged to a different group. After all, this is what the cards and the colours meant. And recognizing that they were tied closer to their classifications than to their proximity and their friendship, the three gave themselves up to a gradually increasing realization that these elements would not stop the separation, accentuated by the cards. Green, blue, yellow . . . blue, yellow, green . . . yellow, green, blue—the colours of the cards were clearly and quickly impressed into their minds, each woman perceiving the differences her colour signified as they began to feel differently about themselves and each other. Finally, like probabilistic data implied by a threatened modification to their convivial relationship, the inkling of differentiation which had begun to divide them since the cards became reality, instilling in them the certainty of an irrevocable division based on the characteristics of their respective groups. Green, blue, yellow . . . blue, yellow, green . . . yellow, green, blue . . . Yes: a new and unexpected prejudice had been established by the cards, as different in their colours as the bearers of the cards, the women, had become. So radical and noticeable in its differentiation criterion did that new and unexpected kind of prejudice appear, that the three now felt that they had been branded—there, each one in her house, in a corner, looking at and re-examining her card. Green, blue, yellow . . . blue, yellow, green . . . yellow, green, blue . . . Those colours were like a stigma. There was no escaping the fact that they had been stigmatized—a stigma which reduced them to distinct entities, isolated by their group characteristics yet, at the same time, egalitarianly integrated according to their social situation into the group each represented. Oh, those colours, each one with her colour which was not only on the card, but in her very being, like something which had physically adhered to her inside and out. Then, possessed by the feeling that the cards' colours, by showing what they were, indicated what they had to be from then on as befitting their defined, liable group status, each let herself be taken over by her distinguishing and particular colour to the point that Teodorico's wife felt more blue with each passing

72

moment, and the cohabitating woman more green, and the third more yellow.

At that moment, seized by an uneasy curiosity, they suddenly rushed out to the sidewalk as though by previously arranged signal. Actually, they had experienced an uncontrollable and simultaneous need to see each other again.

'What's wrong?' said Teodorico to his wife as he saw her hurry by the store.

'Nothing,' she answered.

'Did you put your card in a safe place?'

'Of course.'

When they met on the sidewalk, the three women silently stared at each other, surprised, seeing in each others eyes an expression of relieved discovery: they were still the same. No matter what, in spite of cards which divided them, they returned to the certainty that their amicable friendship would remain untouched. Their feeling of intimacy, which had always brought them together, gradually reasserted itself, overcoming the pressure of circumstance like something which exercises a healing effect on an apparent *fait accompli*: the designation dividing them, the group classification isolating them, the colours distinguishing them. Oh, the colours! Then, as they stood on the sidewalk re-examining one another, all the sensations which had assaulted them in the solitude of their homes, everything they had thought about the colours, everything which the colours had impressed on their spirits during those moments of exacerbated differentiation, suddenly seemed to be a fantasy of foolish fear. After all, the colours were only on the cards. It had been a kind of nightmare.

'Well . . .,' said the woman living with her boyfriend, awkwardly breaking the silence of that unexpected sidewalk meeting.

'Now, every time the authorities ask, we will have to show our cards.'

'I just don't understand why they chose those colours,' said Teodorico's wife.

Nine

If she (Teodorico's wife) didn't understand why they had chosen those colours, in compensation neither did her friends (and neighbours). Along with them many, many other people did not understand it either, perhaps the whole Island population. This was of particular consolation to the three since, as everyone knew and knows, misery loves company—a maxim dutifully applied to the authorities' generalized, colourful ignorance of their motives in giving the cards the colours they did. Besides, the women had more important things to worry about, and that was all they needed: create one more worry by trying to figure out why married women were blue, cohabitating ones, green, and singles, yellow. Now, now, as if it weren't already enough to have to worry about not giving cause for the authorities to eventually accuse them of some group transgression, such as having stepped out of line! They wouldn't be so stupid as to do that, nor would anyone else; the authorities were alert, and, in the name of law and technocratic order, would not tolerate anyone, under any circumstances, daring to step out of line.

Besides, jealous of the technocratic order and clarity (yes, clarity, so that no one who broke the law could try and excuse themselves afterwards by claiming that they did so because they hadn't understood the law), the authorities, as we said, had made things perfectly clear regarding the law and the line.

They had therefore drummed into the peoples' heads, in a clear manner so that they would never forget, the following warning:

'The line, in its social conceptualization, corresponds to norms of communal behaviour established by the law. This means that stepping out of line is equivalent to stepping outside the law. And, as we all know, the act of stepping outside of something is the same as setting oneself outside of that very thing. Thus, whoever breaks the law is, of necessity, outside of it. And this is contrary to the law because, assuming that the law exists so that people will stay within its bounds, the act of crossing these bounds or stepping outside the law presupposes a transgression of said law. Notwithstanding, the law is based on an individual's faithful observance of predetermined obligations toward the law, obligations which the law, in order to make respected that which it established, considers broken from the moment in which they cease to be observed. Therefore, it is the individual's responsibility to faithfully follow the law, under penalty of breaking it, so as not to stop following it. After all, a law is set up to be followed, not to be broken. The law is the law, and whoever breaks it is subject to its sanctions which range from a fine to incarceration depending on the gravity of the transgression. Therefore, since the law establishes a norm of behaviour for the island community to assure order and discipline regarding respect for the law, the easiest way for a member of society to behave within the law is not to step out of line.'

Well. From continually reading the official warning you just read . . . No, no, no, no! First, we must say that this warning (actually, it was an explanation, or better yet, a clarified warning, well, an explanation because it bore the title *Explanation*, and, after all, its purpose was to explain) first, we must say that the *Explanation* was published in the three Island newspapers, with the recommendation that it be cut out and saved so that in case of doubt or lapse of memory, it could be referred to whenever necessary. Well, from continually rereading the *Explanation*, proferred by the authorities regarding the line and the law (and especially after the authorities began to send transgresssors to jail), the people not only had memorized all that the authorities had so clearly explained, but they also firmly believe that under no circumstances should they step out of line if they wanted to live, as they should, within the law. But, the line . . . just where was this line? Better not to ask questions, regardless of their nature or content. Plainly and simply, they should follow the law. As they all knew, forwards and backwards, 'the line, in its social conceptualization, corresponds to norms of communal behaviour established by the law.' Thus, they tried to behave according to its dictates; doing so, they would be within the law and, naturally, in line, out of which they shouldn't step, under penalty of breaking the law.

Thus, if Teodorico's wife was momentarily inquisitive as to the choice of colours for the cards, she quickly renounced the curiousity which could have led her into matters which were none of her business. Prudently, her friends followed her example. As the law determined, their obligation was to remember to carry their cards which identified them as group units within their respective groups. No worrying about the cards' colours, trying to understand why, or seek out an explanation. The simple fact that the authorities had not offered one, clearly indicated that no one should seek the explanation for that which the authorities had not explained—under penalty of breaking the authorities' authority, of breaking the law, in short: stepping over the line. If an explanation had been necessary, the authorities would have given one. Anyway, even if they hadn't given some explanation of the colours, they must have had some reason for choosing them. Who knows? Perhaps a hidden motive . . . But, if there were a motive which the authorities preferred to hide, so much the better that no one wanted to discover it.

Actually, the truth is that the authorities themselves didn't understand the reason for choosing those colours for the cards. (But no one on the Island could know this.) Meeting in the subterranean conference room of the Authorities' Palace, they looked at and re-examined the sketches of the cards (they were still in their preliminary stages), displayed on a panel illuminated by a spotlight. Everything seemed in order: the format, the wording, the graphics layout for the text, dotted lines where the corresponding information would be filled in, the space reserved for the stamp— but . . . why those colours?

76

Then, turning to the specialist in visual communications who, besides having co-participated in the cards' planning, also accompanied their display, standing at the foot of the panel—one expert asked him,

'What did you have in mind by choosing these colours?'

'I had in mind their visual impact,' answered the visual communications specialist.

'Ah, their visual impact . . .' responded the expert, with the air of one who has finally begun to understand the matter.

A second expert, revealing an analytic bent, observed, 'Don't these colours have some symbolic connotation?'

'No,' said the specialist. 'Any idea of symbolism would be significant in a subjective intention which, technically speaking, would be at variance with material treated in strictly objective terms. It was in this last sense that I prepared my work. That is: my work was oriented according to an objective consideration of colours, as visual elements of differentiation, designed to produce, visually, the chromatic effect characteristic of the specific content of each as a colour.'

The authorities glanced momentarily at each other.

'You mean, then, that it is purely a problem of visual impact?' asked the specialist with the analytic spirit.

'Yes. It is a question of visual impact in function of optical focus,' answered the technician, radiating in his turn assurance.

'Ah!' exclaimed some specialists, with awed surprise, while others limited themselves to a grave nodding of heads.

The visual communications specialist proceeded.

'When I choose, for example, the colour green for a cohabitating female, I did not intend to imply any of those old, conventional sentiments which the technocracy eradicated, and which new generations were thankfully spared.'

'You are, perhaps, referring to hope?' asked the oldest authority, a man with grey hair.

'Exactly. Hope was a mystical emotion and, as such, was incompatible with the technocratic reality. In a technocracy, there is no room for abstractions of this type which, in other times, religion inculcated into impoverished souls, falsely promising that if they would only wait with resignation, they could obtain the thing for which they hoped. Besides, hope makes one believe in the existence of personal well-being, created by obtaining the awaited opportunity. In a technocracy, however, as we all know, there is nothing to want for since every honest, licit thing which a person could desire such as an improved standard of living, or personal benefits accrued from being integrated into the general welfare, all this represents absolute, concrete reality. Then, if everything one could hope for already exists in our society, in terms of achieved desires or *realized* dreams, this means that hope has simply ceased to exist. Actually, hope did exist in the technocracy; not, it's clear, as an emotion imbued with resignation and dreamy desire as in its old, mystical-religious concept, but as the act of conquering the status of social well-being from within the framework of order and business. It therefore existed, and only existed, until the moment in which it was supplanted by the reality which overtook it: the reality of the technocratic government, today perfectly equipped to rapidly deal with the problems of the community—wherever, whenever and however they may appear.

(During all this time, the specialist spoke with a burning conviction that there could be no viewpoint other than the one he expressed, since everything he uttered had had to be said. After all, the *Guide for the Good Technician*, which he read every night before retiring, said in one of its passages— 'From the unity of argument, unity of idea'—and it was the duty of every technician to realize that outside of what the *Guide* said, there was nothing to be said. This is what every citizen had to say, not only to himself, but to everyone else until he had convinced them that what he had to say was what the book said.

'Yes, yes . . . I understand,' responded the oldest of the specialists. 'But, in any case, the green colour did suggest to me the possibility of a relationship between it and hope.'

'It was a perfectly understandable reaction,' admitted the specialist. 'Not only for you, an original technician, but for all the Island's authorities who supported the proposal to install the Technocracy on that historic evening of 8 October, known as "The Night of the Final Word"; the idea of a contingent link between the colour green and the feeling of hope could occur not only to you, but even to integral elements of our Corps of Technicians. After all, it's only been two years since the word hope was eliminated from the dictionary. More time must elapse before it will be totally forgotten as it should be.'

The old specialist could not hide his sensitivity to the expert's allusion to his status of 'original technician'. And, giving in to a pleasant feeling of flattered vanity (and, evidently, trying to amend that which now seemed to him— the 'original technician'—to be a nostalgist's lamentable *faux pas*), he smiled, and hurriedly corrected himself.

'Yes, the word hope . . . It was hope, not as an emotion, but as a word, that I thought about when I saw the green card.'

The visual communications expert looked at him for a moment, apparently hesitating, but actually mentally evaluating what he had just heard. The word hope . . . hope as a word . . . Yes, it was quite different! It was no longer a question of a colour, but of a *word*. In this case, the matter was outside of his technical speciality. No problem, however. When a technician did not understand the technicalities of something because that thing was not in his technical speciality, all he had to do was to call on another specialist who specialized in the area outside of the other specialist's speciality, so that he could explain it in his place. The important thing was to have it explained technically. Hadn't the older technician just admitted that he thought of hope as a *word* only? Well, this could be clarified as had happened at the beginning when it was explained how the green colour of the card had nothing to do with hope as a feeling. Little did it matter that he had not formally asked for an explanation of hope as a word, but had only mentioned, as a *word*, hope. Anyway, whatever the motive (and the motive, in this case, was the cards), when the authorities met with the technicians, it was to hear the technicians' explanations. It was their responsibility, therefore, to give their explanations because, as the *Guide to the Good Technician* had established, 'all things require a technical explanation'.

So, following strict techno-professional scruples, the technician turned to the oldest authority.

'Since you thought about hope as a *word*, I will ask my colleague to add to my response. The matter falls within his technical speciality.'

And gesturing toward the other end of the display board, he pointed to a thin man wearing wire-rimmed spectacles, silently following the exposition regarding motives for the cards' colours.

'My pleasure,' answered the second technician, that is, the thin man with the wire spectacles, who began his additional comments.

'As you all know, my colleague and I worked together on planning the cards. I should say that our work was directed towards a communicative summation. He was in charge of chromatic proposals, and I, as specialist in audiographic communication, took charge of textual matters. This means that material relating to the text of the cards was under my supervision since, after all, there was a text to be communicated to the bearers of the cards. Now, my colleague has asked me to add to his answer although, strictly speaking, there isn't an answer to be supplemented, but rather an explanation to be given. An answer, naturally, presupposes the existence of a question which, in this case, doesn't exist. Nonetheless, while there was no *question*, an explanation may contain an answer which is offered or acts as a supplement to a clarification—as long as that clarification, while not directly solicited by a question, circumstantially manifests itself as a result of mentioning reference data. In this case, the reference data was the *word*. Before entering into the explanation *per se*, or the supplement to the answer, I think it would be useful to make a few general remarks concerning audiographic communication which is the area of my technical expertise. Of necessity audiographic communication is based on the production of texts, or rather, on the production of a type of communicative material destined to establish communications via the written word by direct reading of the printed text, or by a second party reading the text in order to reach a third party auditorily through an indirect process of reading—that is, reading communicated via radio and television. In other times, the production of texts, as far as the establishment of communications via the specific and direct consumption of reading matter, was an activity exercised by authors—individuals who, under the guise of narrative fantasy, became rich by instilling dissociated feelings of a personal nature into the masses. In the technocracy, this activity was substituted by audiographic communication which elevated the *word* to a strict utilitarian plane, as a means of inter-communicative expression acting in the interests of informing. Which means that in the technocracy, the *word*, once abused and twisted, was freed of any and all connections with the springs of anxiety and anguish exploited by former authors. Thus, a word began to mean only that which it specifically signified or should signify according to its use and consumption, as a means to produce—communicatively speaking—a determined piece of information. When one says, for example, the word "sweet", the word "sweet" should not be used to produce a stimulus synonomous with "gentle", as authors once did, but only the naturally informative stimulus. That is, the gustatory stimulus, as objective information about a thing sugared by using a "sweet" substance. After all, sweet is that which is sweet or has a sweet flavour. Similarly, the word "green" should not imply anything else than what it means—or expresses—as information about a determined colour. To sum up: the *colour* green is no more than the visual projection of the word "green".'

Having said that, the expert in audiographic communication concluded his explanation or 'supplement to the answer' regarding the green cards.

'Perfect,' said the visual communications technician. 'In terms of a *word*, I believe that the colour green has been sufficiently clarified. From the point of view of my speciality, I need only add that green, as a colour, is simply a colour.'

'Perfect!' cried some authorities.

'There's no doubt that this was a perfect explanation,' said other authorities.

Then, to demonstrate that as an 'original technician', he had profited by the lesson learned from other technicians who taught the authorities what the technocracy was, the oldest authority turned to the specialists.

'Yes . . . yes . . . Perfect! Everything is quite clear and lucid. As a colour, as a word, green is simply green, as yellow is yellow, and blue is blue. Perfect. The cards' colours have been explained.'

'You mean, then, that it all boils down to a question of . . . of visual impact,' said the analytically inclined official.

'Of course!' confirmed the visual communications specialist. 'Objectifying their differential visual impact, I chose the colours based exclusively on their chromatic interest, without seeking to establish any connection between them and the subjective data which might have been suggested by the condition of the card holders. Here is (pointing to one of the sketches on the display montage) a prime example of what I've been saying: this is the card for widows. I choose blood-red and deliberately avoided maroon which, in other times, connoted sadness just as green indicated hope. If in the technocratic society there is no longer any motive justifying hope, there certainly can't be one for sadness. Grief over the death of someone? Yes, in this sense sadness is a permissible emotion, although death should be regarded as a natural phenomenon. Meanwhile, it's not going to be with any exhibitions of semi-mourning maroon that a widow can easily demonstrate her sorrow for the death of her husband. True, legitimate feelings of grief, to be accepted as such, are incompatible with such outward demonstrations. This explains why I choose blood-red instead of maroon for the widows' cards, much less black, the old colour of mourning which, by the way, would make it impossible to see the dotted lines. With this, I hoped to avoid having foolish people eventually relate the colour of the card to the state of widowhood in its varying degrees of mourning: semi- to full. After all, besides having abolished the use

82

of mourning clothes in the technocracy, one must also remember that our great benefactress, donor of Central Institute of Technology's computer system, the Widow Matias M. M. McGregor, who gave the Island community so many edifying examples of technocratic idealism, never, never dressed in mourning.'

'And the card for virgins?' asked the analytical authority.

'This is it,' answered the visual communications specialist, turning to the display montage to point out an ochre card. 'In the case of the virgins' card, I followed the same reasoning as with the widows, as related to the necessity of avoiding any possible suggestion in the colour of personal data of a subjective nature. Therefore, I did not use blood-red which could connote the state of virginity and the sanguinary breaking of the hymen, which physically defines this state. At the same time, I tried to exclude the possible association of this colour with the idea of *danger*, so characteristic of certain persons who, in one form or another, are still chained to the conventionalisms of old, family prudery. Although since the institution of sexual liberty in our society, virginity has ceased to offer any *danger* in terms of extramarital relations, I preferred to use a colour other than blood-red for their cards. And I chose ochre. After all, what interested me was the colour and only the colour, as a function of its specific chromatic content.'

'Yes . . . yes. One must recognize that the virgins' card is perfectly attuned to the idea of visual impact,' commented the analytical authority. 'Ochre is a colour which produces an impact. Even from far away, a person can recognize it. But . . . the card for separated women? What is their colour?'

'Tobacco brown,' answered the visual communication expert.

'But, that's splendid!' cried the analytic authority, intently studying the card which the technician showed him. 'That colour is also one which produces an impact.'

'But suppose their group status changes?' inquired another authority who, silent until then, had resolved to ask something.

83

'In case of change in group,' clarified the technician, 'we will simply exchange cards. This is also duly explained in the text for the cards.'

He turned to his colleague in audiographic communication.

'Would you do us the favour of reading the text?'

'It reads as follows,' said the other, adjusting his wire-rimmed spectacles. 'Safeguard your card, presenting it whenever required to do so. Remember that presentation of this card is the only means you have to prove that you were registered as required by law. In case of change of group status, determined by change in civil status or by change in simple social state equivalent to civil status, present your card to the authorities for the corresponding exchange.'

'Perfect!' cried the authorities.

And they approved the cards which were printed up and later distributed among their corresponding diverse groups according to the colour selected for each.

Finally, when there were no more questions and nothing left to clarify, the authorities adjourned. Colours . . . only colours. Ah! Now the authorities were fully informed as to what the cards' colours signified: they didn't mean a damn thing.

Ten

Everything was done to facilitate the women's registration. No woman would have any difficulties in getting her card. Problems which could occur under other circumstances—time, transportation, scheduling—ceased to exist in view of the appointments schedule set up by the technicians. Apparently, the plan tried to conciliate the law's requirements with the needs of the women by suppressing any and all problems which might hinder them from faithfully complying with the law. The women themselves, in submitting to the registration and in getting the cards, were the first to recognize that although the law required them to do this, it did not require them to sacrifice their creature comforts such as time, transportation, and scheduling. Anyway, there were no problems for any woman in getting her card. Regular housewives, like Teodorico's wife and her friends and neighbours (as we already saw), had only to hop over to the corner—right there, close, only three blocks away at most—to be able to find, strategically located for their convenience, one of the movable registration booths with the men in brown caps distributing and stamping the cards. It was all very easy. Quick and simple. No interrupting domestic chores, catching a bus, going out of the house without knowing when they'd return, all those things. And in the middle of such convenience the important thing was that the law was fulfilled. After all, if the technicians had facilitated the process by suppressing any problem which might hamper the women's registration, they didn't do so just to be occupied, but because they knew what they were doing, and they did it thusly because they knew from technical analysis of cause and effect that when scheduling facilitated registration, registration would facilitate complying with the law. This didn't mean, however, that in the case of unforeseen difficulties arising, the law would cease to be followed.

Meanwhile, although housewives benefited particularly from the registration facilities (the hop to the corner to get the card without risking a burned lunch), the aspect which most worried the technicians from among all the means adopted to facilitate registration was not the number of facilities in specifically residential areas but the level of production. They had received express instructions from the Director regarding this matter. Under no circumstances could the registration be allowed to affect norms of production by interrupting business hours to let women go get their cards. Besides, if all Island women were to be registered, it was only natural that the technicians should be worried, not about a certain area of feminine activity, but about all areas of work in which women participated since, in the end, women did work and, in large measure, levels of production depended on them.

'The means of production cannot interrupt regular business hours as they did during the hospital visits when considerable segments of the feminine work force were immobilized as a consequence of their massive attendance in the hospital lines,' stated the Director to the members of TechTAF (Technical Task Force), in charge of regulating the registration process.

With this, the Director did not mean to imply any technical organizational error in the hospital appointments. On the contrary. Recognizing that the medical examinations were an emergency preventative measure, the Director himself declared it to be a necessary evil which, while it did coincidentally affect the means of production, did so in order to prevent a greater evil: uncontrolled population growth. The lines were slow because they had to be. Let the women be licenced, then. But without hurting production levels. After all, they no longer had to get abortions, just cards.

As he concluded his instructions to TechTAF, the Director added,

'The ball is in your court, gentlemen. I recommend that you maintain a system capable of facilitating the registration

86

of women, and that the legal registration be done without interfering with the women's activities nor with the global production yield of which their activity is a part. Under no circumstances can we permit the registration process to have a negative effect on production levels.'

This was enough to force the technicians to diligently seek a rational solution to the problem. During the problem-solving phase, their first meeting was entirely dedicated to the introduction of treatises. It could not be otherwise since, if there were a task force established with determined goals, the first step in achieving these determined goals would naturally be for the task force to submit the papers they had written. Finally, with the treatises introduced, they set the date for a second meeting. And, in this second session, since there were no more papers to be submitted, the technicians tried to develop the ideas presented at the first meeting. For two hours they discussed them, analysing all the options available for the registration process, in the interests of production levels. No matter what, production levels must not be affected by interrupting office hours, as in having the women leave their place of employment under the pretext of registering. The technicians finally found the only possible solution to the problem, an extraordinarily practical solution which prompted its immediate approbation by the 'analytic unanimity' of the second meeting. The solution was the following: register women at their own place of employment in order to stop them from having a good excuse to leave work and go register at the corner booth.

'The problem is solved,' said one of the technicians of TechTAF for Registration. 'Now all that's left is the scheduling plan, derived from the solution found for the problem. That is: in so far as the problem suggests a solution, the solution will suggest the plan.'

'But, what about solutional problems?' asked a second technician. 'The solution to one problem leads to other problems, which lead to new solutions, solutions which lead to new problems, in the dynamics of solutional problems. Actually, no problem produces a solution without that solution producing new problems.'

'Well, the solutional problems have been duly worked into the plan,' responded the first technician. 'Naturally, we must adopt two types of booths for registration: outside or conventional booths, distributed sectorially throughout the city as a function of block groups or residential conglomerations, and interior or special booths which will operate in the women's places of employment such as factories, industries of all sorts and kinds, well, anywhere there may be a small or large communal, feminine work concentration. Since the domestic sector doesn't interfere with production levels, housewives will be seen at outdoor booths. Production will not suffer in the least from the time a housewife may loose by going to the registration booth. By the same token, outside booths will also serve the maids. With respect to areas of general, non-domestic work, specifically linked to production, registration will take place at interior or special booths set up at the work locations.'

'My colleague refers to the working class, right?' asked a fourth technician.

'I do, and by extension, to all women whose activity in one form or another is linked to production, regardless of professional category or the status one's activity may have,' answered the first technician.

'And white collar workers? Civil servants? Secretaries for commercial firms? Other white collar workers?' insisted the fourth technician who, minutes before, had jotted down the words 'white collar' on the paper in front of him.

'Well . . .' said the first technician. 'Production is an all-inclusive whole, isn't it? Therefore, in its scope, viewing it as a whole, production involves not only those activities directly linked to it, but also those which are indirectly connected. This means that in so far as production depends on industry, industry depends on commercial offices which, in turn, depend on industry, just as industry and commercial firms depend on public funds which exercise a set of controlling actions over the factories and offices: fiscal control, assistance control, salary control, general control of prices, etc. From which one must conclude that without public funds, production would not exist.'

'Well, yes,' the fourth technician finally admitted. 'None-theless, if we accept production as an inclusive whole, we must also recognize that it presupposes the formulation of a set of rules or general principles out of which is shaped a phenomenon, that is, a specific context with its own characteristics and determined constants.'

'A phenomenon is composed of characteristics which define it as such,' observed the first technician.

'Exactly,' answered the other. 'What I mean to say, therefore, is the following: in so far as no phenomenon, in the totality of characteristics of which it is composed, can be analysed without evaluating its characteristic constant, no problem can be conveniently solved without taking into account the necessary parameters.'

'But we already have our parameters,' interrupted one technician.

'And we have our problem,' added another.

'Our problem is registering the women,' concluded a third.

'And the parameter of registration is the level of production,' stated the first technician emphatically.

So there were no more digressions, nor more requests for clarification, nor any more questions raised, nor anything else. A conclusive silence followed, indicating that all the considerations offered for debate had unalterably led them to find in the problem the aforementioned solution. To wit: registration, in places of employment for all women whose activities were linked to production—since, after all, production levels could not be affected under any pretext.

'The problem does not allow any speculative inter-pretation,' finally concluded the President of TechTAF for Registration. If all problems have a nucleus of development, it should be discussed from a progression leading to the achievement of a goal, based on a relationship of intention. This means that if we have a problem to solve, and to resolve it we have our parameters, then the purposes are clear in terms of resolved objectives. Therefore, all that remains is to recommend what should be done. And what should be done, according to the sense and objective of the problem and the set of co-ordinates implying its solution, is, in a word, to adopt a means of tacit relevance to resolve it. If the problem is to safeguard production levels, and there is no way to do so without interfering with business hours, obviously production will be safeguarded only if the women, in order to comply with the registration law, do not leave their place of employment during this time.'

And with these words, he closed the debate and, immediately thereafter the session, having read and approved the recommendation, quickly sent it to the Director with the conclusions reached—without risk to production levels—by TechTAF, charged with solving the problem of registering women whose activities were directly or indirectly linked to production.

Eleven

'What's that?'

'How are they going to do it?'

These were the questions that many women asked each other as they walked to work that morning (to factories, to offices, to stores, etc., but mainly to factories). With orderly and conformist curiosity, they found that the registration would be in their own places of business. Still, there were some doubts as to the time that registration would occur. Would it be right at the start of work when you signed in, or punched the time clock? Or would it be after hours? This last hypothesis was not particularly appealing to them since, when they left work tired and in a hurry, all they wanted to do was to catch the bus and quickly get home. They weren't made of steel. But they had only to wait till they got to work, and everything was made perfectly clear, although with a possible surprise for them. Concerned with production levels, the authorities had determined that registration would take place during lunch. There was an announcement tacked to the wall explaining everything. The customary hour lunch break would be reduced to 30 minutes, reserving the other half hour for registration. They would have to eat quickly because after the 30 minute lunch period, a bell would ring to signal the start of registration which, under no circumstances, was to exceed the other half hour, at the close of which the customary signal would be given to indicate the resumption of work. Not counting, of course, the first signal which indicated the start of lunch. Besides, obedient to the programmed schedule which no industry could interrupt for lunch, the factories' signal to resume work had a cumulative function, indicating the rotation of 'lunch shifts' by signalling the end of lunch for the first shift and, at the same time, the beginning of lunch for the second. Hence, there was a lunch shift from 11 to 12, and another from 12 to one, both staggered according to their starting date of work in the factory in order to avoid complaints, the pesterings of any worker (we're speaking of women) who judged herself to have been overlooked in her hunger. Those who ate last had to resign themselves to the fatal recording of the number they had received when they were hired.

The routine of these signals was interrupted by the introduction of the extra (or intermediate signal indicating the registration hour. Nonetheless, given its temporary character, this noisy provision would only last as long as registration.

The technicians had recommended another very practical measure which, in the interests of harmonizing the dynamics of registration with the time (30 minutes) alloted for it, was adopted by the authorities on an emergency-obligatory basis. The provision consisted of the following: personnel departments would be in charge of filling in the cards beforehand with data they already had in their personnel files; the women would then only have to sign and pick up their cards, wasting only a minimum amount of time, even if they did have to occasionally add some additional information.

In their analysis the technicians had classified the signals as audiowarnings, to make it very clear that it was not a question of luminous warnings, but signals (or warnings) designed to produce specifically auditory control effects. It's fortunate that at this time we remembered this important clause of the analysis since the authorities expressly referred to it when they condescended (in the registration directive) to allow factory owners to use the audiowarning which was most convenient or which was already 'conventionally installed as a system'. To wit; bell, gong or siren, operating in perfect synchronization with local office time clocks, duly set to the Official Time signalled every five minutes by ASERT (Amalgamated Services for Radio Transmission) in conjunction with DECCT (Department for Control of Chronological Time). In case it was impossible to register all employees during the allotted 30 minutes, the operation would be repeated on subsequent days for as long as necessary to conclude the registration process, excluding the hypothesis of extending the lunch schedule.

(To clarify, registration was limited to the lunch hour because the night shift, when and where it was necessary, was staffed exclusively by men. Women don't work at night. Taking advantage of this comprehensive and agreeable measure taken by the authorities, the Island's feminine work force, while they had to eat lunch at work, could go serenely home to eat dinner.)

Thus, on a certain date and thereafter for eight or ten days, the registration audiowarnings stridently resounded at the appointed hour, causing extra movement during the lunch schedule, with women hurriedly abandoning the lunch tables to hurriedly throw themselves into the search for their cards.

'Get in line!' shouted the personnel clerk.

Still chewing, many of them took their place in line, anxiously waiting to be seen during the half hour allotted for registration. If they weren't, they would have to eat with the same speed the next day and return to the line again until they finally got their cards.

'Hurry up! Hurry up!' ordered the clerk, stamp in hand. 'Sign quickly. There are still lots of people who have to sign.'

And to provide the proper example of speed he required, the clerk imposed an energetic, rapid rhythm on his work, stamping the cards before the ink was barely dry and diligently stacking them up with his other hand before he had hardly finished stamping them.

Then, raising his impatient stamp into the air, he would shout to the next woman.

'You! Let's go! Hurry up and sign!'

Sometimes, faced with what seemed to him to be a delay, he would mutter.

'God! What a long name you have!'

Nonetheless, even with whim's occasional aggravations and the snail-like calligraphy, he did not ease the requirement that they sign their full name on the card because that was what the law mandated, be the name fortuitously short or exaggeratedly long.

Finally, when the agreed 30-minute audiowarning would sound, the clerk, attentive to the interruption, would irrevocably lay the stamp down on the table and, involving the remaining registrants in a superior state of assessment, he would again shout out.

'Come back tomorrow, in order! And now, back to work!'

Docile to his command, the women would silently go to work while another line formed for the second and last shift. And so, there still being women to register, the operation successively repeated itself, always the same as the first day: the lunch break cut in half, the other half dedicated to registrations—with signatures, shouts, and stampings. Until one day, the last registerable woman in the Island's largest factory had been registered, and registration in places of business was concluded, having safeguarded—as the technicians had foreseen—production levels. (Registration at outdoor booths, thanks to an extended schedule, had finished three days earlier.) The receipt of this important information did not stop the Director from worrying about some special data of programmatic control. After all, if facts were controlled through programming control data, it was natural that he be satisfied only after verifying that no fact was uncontrolled—and this was a special fact, requiring special control.

'What about the Domestic Commandos?' the Director asked of one of the CCOSMOS technicians (Council for the Co-ordination of Special Missions). 'Have all the Commandos been paid?'

'All Domestic Commandos have completed their missions. The last one of them just sent a message to Command Central confirming the fact,' answered the advisor. And he proceeded with other matters he considered pertinent.

'The DCs, or Domestic Commandos, played a totally positive role, whether in the productivity of each in particular or in the total result of their specific missions. Thanks to the actions of the DCs, all the women in the interior have been registered, even in those areas which still lack business administrative organization. In carrying out their missions, they reviewed all the ranches, farms and agricultural villages. This naturally was facilitated by our perfect assessment services carried out by PAPA (Programme for the Assessment of the Population's Activities). Thanks to PAPA, as you know, there is not one Island inhabitant, even those living in the remotest corner, who has not been duly assessed, indicating their address and the specific activity engaged in. The efficiency of the registration of women carried out in the interior by the DCs, in the aforementioned areas still lacking business administrative organization, or SD Areas, in sum, can only be compared with the actions undertaken by those same DCs in said areas during the obstetrical examinations.'

'We can never emphasize enough the importance of the DC's actions regarding that event,' interrupted another technician from CCOSMOS. 'On that occasion, I inspected some of those areas, and I can give my personal assurance as to their efficiency. In SD Areas, there are no hospitals. . . .'

'Not only in SD Areas, but in similar microregions,' added a second technician, jealous of the fact.

'Yes . . .' responded the other. 'There are still no hospitals in those areas, only Medical Outposts which meanwhile satisfiably substitute for the lack of hospitals, performing 16,200 abortions out of the 33,180 women lined up by the DCs for the obstetrical examination. Thus, the DCs did much more than act as a support team in arranging for examinations at the Medical Outposts. In hospital trucks conveniently staffed by medical personnel, they canvassed the most remote of SD Areas and similar microregions, covering locales lacking even a simple Medical Outpost. And in those hospital trucks, in spite of scarce supplies, borne up by a laudable spirit of teamwork and a perfect understanding of the gravity of the problem of the population explosion, the DCs performed with absolute success nothing less than 18,352 abortions. This is a socio-statistical fact of extraordinary import which should never be forgotten from the page of services performed for the community by the DCs, in the dynamics of their work and versatility of action—versatility of action which once again was as evident in one event as in the other: in the case of the obstetrical examinination, they knew how to adjust themselves to a level of compatibility with the necessities of their spheres of operations, inviting the indispensible collaboration of the doctors, just as, with propriety and operational tact, they ,knew how to recruit elements necessary from the Brown Cap Guard to carry out, in these same areas, the group registration of women. Still, in these two events, it is necessary to praise the organizational skills of CCOSMOS which, as an organ for the co-ordination of special missions, has, after Command Central, responsibility for the formation and direction of the DCs.'

'The DC's actions derive from two sources: CCOSMOS and Command Central,' observed the first technician. 'But the important thing is that all Island women have been registered according to their social group, to carry out their division into groups.'

'Good,' interrupted the Director. 'Now that all Island women have been duly registered, including those which previously had had the gynecological examination in order to figure into the obstetrical assessment, this means that the grouping of women, recommended by the group technicians as a preventative control measure for the initiation of Operation Violet, is finally over. In this case, only one thing is left for the government to do: immediately begin Operation Violet for the well-being of all and the social security of the Island.'
the rest of the summoned council members, amidst a conclusive scraping of chairs. Then, exchanging the technocratic salute (fist raised, thumb up) with his advisors, the Director dismissed them and concluded the meeting.

Twelve

The women in the SD areas (a euphemistic abbreviation for Subdeveloped) and the corresponding microregions had hardly said goodbye to the hospital trucks when the DCs returned in other vehicles, with different objectives and different personnel: or, rather, a new mission charged to new personnel who had so quickly brought in a new novelty—oh, what a novelty! a rare commodity on those distant isles.

The first time, they saw men in white aprons: after all, they were doctors and nurses. The doctors were on the mission we already know about: examine the women and, if called for, give them an abortion in compliance with the mandatory three month abortion law—a period which the text of said law referred to as 'abortive privation'. And, so that there was no doubt that it was a legal measure, and to avoid having anyone think that the doctors were acting illegally, the local guards gave the doctor's actions the necessary legal backing of their automatic pistols, as instructed by the directive. This precaution was considered indispensible since the law, in order to command obedience, had to convincingly demonstrate its power of repression, ready to be exercised in case of non-compliance. Since pistols serve the law, there is no law without guns. Everyone on the Island was perfectly aware of this—but it was still necessary to show them the guns in some form or another.

The second time they saw the men in the brown caps, their simple presence was independent of the collaboration of local authorities the better to convince the community that they were there in the name of the law. Besides, they were known agents of the law, and as such they also carried automatic weapons. They had come to supervise the registration of the women, as they explained over their cars' loudspeakers, also confirming what had been fully publicized

97

by the radio and TV. Widely distributed literature explained the details of the adopted registration criteria to those directly concerned, that is, to the women, and to those indirectly concerned (husbands, relatives and/or parents of the women).

The cars used in the two actions were also different, as the actions themselves were different, each one claiming, because of their specific objectives, a suitable type of vehicle except, of course, for the licence plates which remained the same: on the egalitarian slate grey of official plates, only their numbers differed. (The numbers were yellow.)

The first time, they saw hospital trucks pulling spacious aluminium trailers equipped with antiseptic examining rooms and operating tables. The second time, the trailers had been replaced by huge vans containing metal file cabinets to house the cards. The cards were divided according to PAPA's specifications (name, address, activity) and according to the determinant group colour to effectuate the registration and the group division of the women. It's clear that no one would profit by trying to escape registration because, with PAPA's assessment specifications, the men in the brown caps had all the women under rigorous control. Anyway, the Island's feminine community was so conscious of the responsibility of their role in the government's efforts to control the rising birthrate, that there was no woman in any SD Area or corresponding microregion who would not let herself be registered, just as previously none of them hesitated in having the doctors examine them. It must also be said that although they were exempt from the examination and the registration, the men were no less conscious than the women of the necessity of birthcontrol as proclaimed by the authorities. Actually, during the panicy intimacy of the uncontrolled birthrate, all the Island population faced the problem with a clear awareness of the alternative offered: stop making babies, or die of starvation.

After the registration vans departed, the SD Area and corresponding microregion women were left wondering about what new thing was to come down the road, brought in by different vehicles and different DCs. They had already been examined, registered—and now, what else could the government want them to do so that they would be doing what it wanted? For a few days, they gave in to an uneasy anticipation caused by a kind of frustrated curiosity, a frenzy of useless speculation. And now, what would happen? They didn't know, although everything led them to an inevitable conclusion which seemed absolutely logical: if the government had mobilized the women to control the exploding birthrate, then it must have something else in mind for them to do to perfect what it had already done with their participation. It was clear that the government, so preoccupied with practical measures, wasn't going to indefinitely submit women to abortions, nor let them exchange cards indefinitely. Sooner or later, the government would end up taking some more practical measure. Besides, the government was zealous enough about their planning strategies that they wouldn't put two preliminary measures into effect— the obligatory three month abortion and the group registration—without first having ready an additional one to complement the first two. It was merely a question of time. All in all, the women didn't have long to wait for the government's new measure, announced to them in terms of a definitive solution to the problem, with all the requirements for a denouement, complete and finished, and which gave form and sense to the previous measures while, at the same time, putting an end to it all. It wasn't for nothing that the government, when it announced the new measure, gave it the name of 'The Final Measure'. Then, not only the SD Area and corresponding microregion women, but also all women on the Island, understood that they wouldn't have to expect anything else from the government as far as measures to control the rising birthrate. The problem was definitively solved with 'The Final Measure', announced a few days later.

Thirteen

'The Final Measure' had been announced? This meant that the Director, as he had declared before the convened assembly, had done the only thing that remained for the government to do after the conclusion of the group registration for women: initiate Operation Violet—giving it its true name.

Let's tell you how this name change came about.

Actually, everything was ready for the initiation of the Operation: rigorously developed, meticulously planned—on paper and in secret as the topical prevention and control technician had recommended. It lacked only the Director's go-ahead, at the opportune time, to put into effect all that had been on paper and until then, kept in secret, known only to those technicians who had written the Contraceptive Strategem (CONSTAT) under the codename of Operation Violet. After all, no plan can be executed without first having a paper where people can project the reality into which the plan will be converted, which means (as one of SUPERCAP's technicians pointed out), that the paper, from the moment it contains a plan, 'is the state prior to the planned reality'. It wasn't for nothing that SUPERCAP had a sign with this warning: *If you have a plan, put it down on paper*. Thus, being what it was—a body charged with producing and/or evaluating plans—SUPERCAP used more paper as new plans were suggested; it was natural that it should use a lot of paper to produce and evaluate the plans. The Director himself, infused with the planning spirit which also dominated all other governmental departments, never gave up this fundamental norm. When someone would sound him out about an idea, he would invariably answer,

'It's an idea. But where's the plan?'

And there went more paper.

100

Paper for paper, Operaton Violet's planning consumed 58 pages, typewritten on both sides. The pages were collected into a black notebook equipped with a metallic pressure clasp to keep them in a solid, neat stack. A white sticker was glued to the cover where, in blue italic printing, one could read: *Operation Violet*. Picking up the notebook, the General Co-ordinator wrote on the sticker in large, threatening red letters: SECRET! (With exclamation and everything.) Afterwards, accompanied by two other advisors, he took the notebook to the Director to give him the final, overall briefing for the plan, backed by audiovisual projections of the accompanying charts. (Until then, the plan still bore the name CONSTAT.) The General Co-ordinator talked on and on and, naturally, projected the charts onto a screen especially set up for this purpose. Everyone already had the plan down pat. After all, they hadn't done anything else for the last 28 days except work on it. Nevertheless, possessed by a complete technical satisfaction of authorship, reviewing the plan with the Director, even after having seen it so many times among themselves, gave them a sudden and new professional euphoria, a certainty that no other group, even KIT, under any circumstances, could have done a better job.

Once the presentation was over, the General Co-ordinator considered it indispensable to offer some further clarifications to the Director.

'Please be aware, Mr Director, of the fact that all the alternatives were evaluated in terms of their interest to the analytic nucleus. After all, in developing any plan, one must evaluate all the alternatives so that, in evaluating them, they can be defined as to their degree of interest to the plan. It is clear that, in so far as the alternatives are defined, the plan itself can be re-evaluated with a view to its total definition. This is what happened with Operation Violet. It was continually re-evaluated each time the alternatives were not defined as being at a compatible level with the plan as a whole—since, after all, Operation Violet is a plan. It is a plan—and this can never be overemphasized—which can only be defined as such from the moment in which the

101

evaluation of its totality corresponds to an inter-relationship of valid alternatives, leading inevitably to a single objective. Which means that a plan becomes valid in so far as the alternatives for its execution maintain a level of equivalence, preserving such a strong unity of efficiency that each alone, and all together, assure a totality of action which is, at the same time, multiple and converging, without which no plan can be successfully implemented.'

For a moment, the Director waited for the General Co-ordinator to add something further. The General Co-ordinator, however, had nothing further to say, and this was made very clear when—with the noble, relaxed air of one who has just said everything necessary in absolutely perfect form—he pushed the microphone away and sat down.

Then, in the ensuing silence, everyone turned their eyes toward the Director, in reverent expectation of his pronouncement. Without hesitation, he began.

'Whether from its dialectical aspect or its structural aspect, the plan seems to be perfect to me. There is no doubt but that it will lead to a definitive solution to the problem. Thus, I not only approve it, I also order its immediate implementation.'

A wave of applause interrupted him.

'One moment, one moment!' he cried, raising his arm. The applause obediently stopped.

'There is one more important consideration to make with respect to the declarative construction of the plan's name. The declarative construction of the name of a plan naturally causes perceptual stimuli which should have a permanent correspondence with the message that the plan's name intends to communicate in expressed declarative terminology. In other words: the name of a plan created as a function of the final measure of a problem's solution should be constructed in the sense of a direct, open declaration related to the nature of the measure required by the problematic situation. Therefore, now that Operation Violet as a plan to control the birthrate, is at the level of a final measure, its true name, maintained in secret until now, should be reformulated with a view to a self-definition of what it declaredly

102

is and proposes. That is: the final measure in the solution to a problem. From now on, therefore, the name of the plan will be exactly that which the plan proposes as a solution to the problem: 'The Final Measure'.

At first, some technicians seemed not to understand. There was a rapid exchange of questioning glances. Then, suddenly, everyone understood when the Director, pushing the black notebook to the General Co-ordinator, said in a tone of voice decidedly and sufficiently loud enough to be heard throughout the room, although out of the reach of the microphone,

'Write it there: "The Final Measure".'

And thus it was that the Contraceptive Strategy, camouflaged for nearly a month (for preventative measures) under the codename Operation Violet, ended up by changing its name.

Fourteen

The advisors left the Director's office for that of the General Co-ordinator in accord with the work routine customarily followed after the Director formally approves a plan, beginning with the change of office for a new meeting since, after a plan was formally approved and on its way to becoming law, a meeting in the Director's office inevitably led to another meeting in the office of the General Co-ordinator. A simple question of normative dynamics, as they all knew, and which we will now understand: all plans create a normative dynamic equating its execution to the reality it projects regarding a determined situation, with a view to promoting, according to the nature of its constituent components, the substitution of the previous situation by a new situation, without which it could not be implemented as a plan.

It was in function of that normative dynamic that they began the meeting of which we speak.

In the immense office there was a huge, rectangular table with an impeccably polished top, 15 chairs to a side, and, at the head, a chair with a back higher than that of the others to indicate that the head of a table is not always sufficient to denote a special place at a conference table—unless there were a chair with a higher back there, accentuating the hierarchical importance of the seat.

The General Co-ordinator sat in this chair, placing on the table the black notebook which he had tucked under his arm. One by one, the advisors sat in the other chairs in front of individual desk sets, arranged in irreproachable order, complemented by fountain pens for personal notations.

'Gentlemen!' began the General Co-ordinator. 'As you all know, the Director has just approved the plan contained in this folder.'

He opened the portfolio.

'Then, if we have an approved plan, we must now proceed with the customary formalities, as the law mandates. In other words, to what was approved as a whole, or rather, to the content which was the object of approval, we must now give the prerequisites indispensable to the validity of its implementation, so that what was approved legally can be legitimately executed as the law commands. Naturally, given the gravity of the problem which the plan intends to resolve, this work will have to be undertaken in urgent session. The plan now has a definitive name. Upon terminating the strategic camouflaging precautions of its codename, observed in strictest secrecy until the conclusion of the plan, this name was adopted as a substitute for the name which the plan should have had, but didn't. Thus, after dropping its codename and having had a name by which it should have become known, the plan ended up by taking a name which it did not have, exactly when the codename under which it had been disguised should have given away to public revelation of its true name, which meanwhile will not occur inasmuch as its real name is no longer true because of the substitution of a definitive name, leading to the fact that its real name was only provisionally true, or simply became temporary in so far as the codename was provisionary until the moment in which, ceasing to be the real name, it was substituted by the definitive name which became, naturally, the plan's true name.'

'Would you permit me an observation?' asked one of the advisors. (He was a technician in organizational norms of service and systems.)

'Of course!'

'With great attention I followed the dialectical presentation which you made concerning the procedural change in the plan's name. And I must say that the Director, in giving the plan the definitive name of "The Final Measure", acted in terms of perfect nominative appropriateness. No other name, much less that initially adopted by consensus of SUPERCAP, could be better suited to the proposals and objectives of the plan than this: "The Final Measure".

Besides, if the means previously adopted to fight the rising birthrate proved insufficient, and a new measure was developed, then in terms of the definitive solution to the problems, this means that the problem, once solved by these new means, will find its terminus in them. Then, if the new measure proves able to put an end to the problem, thus eliminating the need to adopt other means, it is, to all intents and purposes, the final measure.'

'Yes, without a doubt,' interrupted a second advisor. 'Either a thing is final or it isn't. And the measure, as it is structured in the plan, involves in its information and consequence, a valid significance as final measure.'

'By the way,' continued the General Co-ordinator, 'after this meeting the plan will always be referred to by its true name. That is: "The Final Measure". Nor is there any more motive for not doing so. The secret cover-up which determined as a preventative measure the use of a false name for the plan during its development, has obviously ceased since the plan's approval by the Director. After all, a plan is only approved after being conclusively developed. Therefore, in so far as the plan is concerned, there are no more developmental problems, only ones of implementation. Thus, it rests with this council to give the plan the legal instrumentation by which it will be executed according to the formalities of law. Then, if the plan has approval and all that we must do is make it conform to the legal formalities necessary to its execution, one cannot but refer to it by its true name, inasmuch as it will be implemented with its real name.'

'Perfect!' said another advisor while the others, in an attitude of grave approbation, slowly nodded their heads.

'But, as I already emphasized, our work requires urgency,' continued the General Co-ordinator. 'After all, the worst is over. I am referring, naturally, to the developmental phase of the plan. Let us, then, without wasting time, try to regulate its execution according to the formal legal requirements. Or, more correctly, in accord with technical appropriateness, since nothing is formulated nor developed which is not a function of a determined technique. As an

106

idea, in order to become a plan, requires an adequate technical development, so a plan becomes law only through the adjustment of its content to the norms of technical, complementary legal formulation.'

A pause, as he slowly flipped through the pages of the plan. Then, with formulatory discipline, he began to instruct the attentive assembly.

'In the first place, we have the definition of the plan's legal nucleus used to formulate the decree under which the plan will be executed, with the law's needed backing. Once accomplished, we can proceed to the regulation of the decree since no decree can enter into force without first having rules. That's the decree technique. Anyway, as you gentlemen know, the regulation of a decree lies in its complementary detailing, in terms of a unified, decreed whole. This is because, in so far as a detail complements a decree, the regulation of a decree purports to establish, within a legal totality, the necessary intercomplementary network which should exist between the structure of a decree and the decree which engendered it. Now, in accord with the operational dynamics of decrees, and not just with its normative dynamics, a decree is structured around an outline of the law, which is to the law's design as such, as the law's design itself is to the law as such. From which one must conclude that the regulation of a decree can only be translated into law after adjusting its outline to the design of the law itself, which, once approved and finally translated into law, will begin to have legal effects, thus assuring the concomitant viability of the decree and of the law which regulates it. Having established this, I now declare that within one hour and forty-five minutes, the Council on Legislation and Norms will have formulated, according to the approved plan, the articles that serve as a base for the implementation, that is, the decree. And, since there is no time to waste, I declare this session to be closed; the rest of the members of this assembly will meet again in one hour and forty-five minutes in this same room.

Fifteen

Ten or 15 minutes after the respective constituent members entered CLAN's offices, the door opened once again to admit a waiter dressed in a black and white uniform, pushing a cheerful teatrolley where—amidst gleaming dishes of silver and porcelain—a platter of cookies, cakes and jellies beckoned. (Evidently, tea had been ordered via the intercom.) Soon afterwards the waiter reappeared minus his equipment and, quickly hurrying out, retraced the carpeted itinerary which had brought him there. After 30 minutes (more or less), evidently summoned by a new intercom call, he returned to the office and quickly removed the teatrolley and some stained napkins crumpled over the remains of the snack. Finally, worried about even a five minute delay, CLAN's members left the office relieved of their important duty. Not counting the time spent in their break, they only had a little more than an hour to finish the work as such. But, although the time was short, they did know how to make it conveniently productive. After all, the idea had already matured, clearly defined in the plan's proposals and objectives, so that all they really had to concern themselves with was the editing of the decree, into which—it must be recognized—they threw themselves with persistence and appetite. When they returned to the General Co-ordinator's office, the rest of SUPERCAP's members were there waiting for them and—logically—for the General Co-ordinator himself.

'I have the honour of presenting you with the minutes of the decree,' said the President of CLAN to the Co-ordinator, giving him the paper which he triumphantly held in his hand.

As a matter of protocol, the General Co-ordinator waited until CLAN's members had taken their seats at the table. When he finally saw them seated in their respective chairs, he began.

'Since all the members of this council are present, I declare the session to be open.'

He paused while he silently read the minutes of the decree, and then continued.

'In accordance with what was established in our previous session, and pursuant to our work, I have the honour of submitting to the assembly the decree formulated by the members of the Council on Legislation and Norms. It is, obviously, in the form of a memorandum which I will now read for the advisors' due appreciation.'

Slowly, he read what was on the paper.

'The Final Measure

The Director, using the powers conferred upon him by the Supreme Technocratic Administration, decrees:

That for the non-deferrable period of 4 (four) decades, the birth of children will be categorically prohibited in all parts of the Island.

That any woman, regardless of social condition or profession, who infringes upon the precepts of this law will be brought before a firing squad.

That the present decree will enter into law on the date of its publication, hereby revoking any previous statutes to the contrary.'

He finished the reading.

'Will all those opposed to the text of the decree please stand.'

Everyone remained seated.

'May I have the floor?' asked a specialist in economics data projections, suddenly breaking the silence which complemented the assembly's solid, overall posture of agreement.

'You have the floor,' answered the deputy general.

'It's obvious that I agree with the memorandum,' said the other, with an evident air of worry. 'The simple fact that I remained seated indicated this. Nonetheless, I would like to propose an alternative phrasing for the expression 'brought before a firing squad''.'

Everyone looked at him with surprise.

'I'll explain,' he said, noting the reaction his words provoked. 'Although I may not believe in the possibility of deliberate transgressions, given the severity of punishment, I admit that many women, through pure ignorance, may be led to unconsciously break the law. Specifically, I am thinking of the women in the SD Areas and the corresponding microregions where the level of social awareness is admittedly low, and where they have not yet recorded a satisfactory mean for the indexes of dimensional information. In sum, given the socio-informative retardation of these areas, cases of involuntary breaking of the law could occur there, at least during the first few months of the law's enactment.'

'The renowned advisor's worry is well taken,' said the General Co-ordinator. 'But, as we have done in similar situations, let us leave it to the Domestic Commandos. They will carry the information to those areas.'

'That does not invalidate the proposition I wish to make,' responded the expert in economics data projections. 'The decree involves data which are so cumulative, and repressive effects which are so imperative, that the DC's actions, while carried out with their usual promptness, may not be exercised at a level of urgency sufficient to prevent the consummation of an anti-economic volume of shootings in the cited areas. After all, a shooting, in its inherent orthodox apparatus, implies high operational costs into which figure not only the expenses of specific types of ammunition, but above all, personnel expenditures such as the formation and relocation of a platoon in charge of carrying out the decree.'

'Your presentation is absolutely correct,' intervened the technician in financial systems and subsystems analysis, in a rapid aside. 'But, what do you propose in the sense of correcting the negative effects of the shootings, as expressed as a budgetary item?'

'I propose a substitution,' answered the other.

At last he was about to reveal the substitution which he had intended to propose from the beginning.

'Instead of "brought before a firing squad", as is in the memorandum, I propose that the decree read: "punished by

110

death''. It is a more flexible criterion which, without compromising the punishment, will permit the use of more economic means to assure the decree's full implementation. After all, there are more economical means of punishing someone by death. Brute force, for example, or one simple shot to the back of the head.'

'Or electrocution,' remembered one of CLAN's members.

'I wouldn't say electrocution, because that involves the cost of electric energy,' argued the author of the substitution. 'For the same reason I have excluded being burned at the stake which, besides constituting obvious hardship to the Service for the Preservation of the Remaining Forests, also requires the use of ancillary inflammable substances which are currently quite expensive due to the price rise and shortage of petroleum.'

'Let's not forget the club,' mused the technician in topical prevention and control. 'One good knock on the head, if vigorously applied, can assure that the foreseen punishment will be carried out with the advantage, admittedly crude, of not involving expense of any kind. In my opinion, the use of the club should be considered.'

'Just a minute,' said the General Co-ordinator. 'We could speculate indefinitely on the means of punishment by death. I consider it to be superfluous to worry about them. Therefore, I ask the advisors to attend to the proposed substitution, which will now come before you for the vote. The question: punished by firing squad or by death? Will all those who approve of the substitution please remain seated.'

Again, no one stood up.

'Since everyone is in agreement, the motion is approved,' said the General Co-ordinator.

And picking up a fountain pen, he carefully crossed out the words 'brought before a firing squad' and added 'punished by death', leaving in the period. For a moment, he forgot everything in the joy of that expeditious grammatical utilization: he was a meticulous soul who could not have ignored the fact that the period had already been typed in, and therefore should stand approved.

Then, he again turned to the members of SUPERCAP.

111

'I will read the passage, now duly amended, since I think that it is of interest that you gentlemen take note of its final, edited form.'

He began.

'Any woman, regardless of social condition or profession, who infringes upon the precepts of this law will be punished by death.'

'Perfect!' cried some advisors, while others limited themselves to the customary head nodding.

'Well, gentlemen,' said the General Co-ordinator. 'Now that the memorandum has been approved, I must now submit it to the Director for his final consideration. After all, we only approved the memorandum. Only the Director can approve it as a decree and give it its corresponding sanction. Therefore, we will meet again in an hour and . . .'

'Will you permit one last question?' asked the specialist in topical prevention and control.

'Ask your question, but please make it brief.'

'Of course. I'll be brief. All I want to know is the following: in the end, what will be the means of death adopted to punish lawbreakers?'

The General Co-ordinator folded the memorandum as he clarified.

'That is a matter for the regulation of the decree. Nonetheless, as you know, the firing squad had definitely been excluded.'

He stood up.

'I hereby declare a 90 minute recess. We will meet again in two hours. Please be prompt as it looks like our work will carry on into the night.'

The room quickly emptied itself. The advisors filed out in silence. Based on a strict sense of official duty, one thought only was uppermost in their minds: the death sentence leading to the sacrifice of some lives was actually insignificant when compared with saving from death by starvation a whole population whose lives were threatened by the rising birthrate. Nonetheless, they were confident that the law—given its severity—would not be broken by a significant number of incidents.

Sixteen

The Director carefully read the decree's memorandum, mentally reviewing each word; and while he mentally reviewed them, he let his head nod with every passing word, as though each mentally ponderous word were actually bearing down upon his head: it was a solid, silent form of approbation. Nonetheless, he had some doubt when he saw the handwritten alteration between the lines.

'Why did you cross out "brought before a firing squad" and put in "punished by death"?'

The General Co-ordinator summed up the arguments which had determined that subtle yet practical substitution.

The Director nodded his head again.

'Ah . . . yes . . . Very good. The arguments are totally cogent. There is no doubt that they were well thought out. Yes . . . yes. Good. Very good.'

He returned the memorandum to the General Co-ordinator.

'Have the decree typed up immediately as it is written in the memorandum. I want to sign it right away. There is no time to lose.'

The General Co-ordinator quickly left the Director's office without, however, failing to reconcile haste with protocol. He returned to his own office, now empty, sat down at the desk and, pressing the corresponding, direct-line electric button, called for the presence of the head of the Mechanographics Section. Examining the luminous controls, he corroborated the fact that the buzzer had sounded in the indicated location—a yellow-orange light gleamed on the small panel in the silent office. Speedily, the control light was joined by the presence of the Mechanographics clerk in a perfect demonstration that the human control was in exact synchronization with the electric control mechanism,

113

activated by the button. Although he was familiar with the rapid effects produced by the control buttons, the General Co-ordinator experienced a moment of visible joy when he verified that only a fraction of time, perfectly compatible with the urgency of the case, had passed between the call and the presence of the clerk. Surely he had gained a few seconds of time by the clerk's speed and this was of extreme importance to him. Rapidly he gave him the necessary mechanographic instructions, and the man left, quickly returning with the decree typed on the correct paper, with the six customary copies. After all, the text of the decree was not so long that it could possibly interfere with the speed of the typists.

He put the decree in a folder (the pages impeccably arranged) and took it to the Director. Caught up by the urgency of the process, the Director signed it 'on the spot', initialling the copies immediately.

He put the fountain pen back in its holder.

'Now, try to get the decree's regulations prepared. SCAN is on duty, waiting to hand out the material tomorrow to the press, radio and TV. After all, it is a notice of supreme importance to the Island, and everyone on the Island should be aware of it.'

'Don't worry, Mr Director,' said the General Co-ordinator. 'The notice will receive the widest possible publication, in accord with the plan developed by SCAN for amalgamated broadcast. There is a complete outline of amassed information ready to be transmitted at the opportune moment. We will initiate an electrifying operation, mobilizing all means of communication.'

The Director had no reason to doubt the efficiency of the plans for broadcasting. Besides, he had known of them before and had approved them. Nonetheless, he was careful to emphasize the fact.

'What I want is for the news, in one form or another, to reach the eyes and ears of all the Island's population.'

'Don't worry, Mr Director,' repeated the General Co-ordinator. 'SCAN will make sure that not only the news of the decree, but the text itself, and, word for word, that of the rules, will reach the eyes and ears of every person on the Island.'

He got up.

'Inside of three hours, in perfect co-ordination with the time set by SCAN, the regulations of the decree will be in your hands.'

Then having put the decree back in the folder, he quickly picked it up, tucked it under his arm, and hurried out of the office. As had occurred in similar circumstances, after leaving the Director's office, he went to his own. Within a few minutes, using the electric buttons, he had called together all of SUPERCAP's members. The new meeting was about to begin.

Until now, dear reader, you and I have had a small advantage—small, but significant—over the people on the Island. No one on the Island (except the technicians who had worked on the plan in absolute secrecy, and, of course, the Director who knew all), no one on the Island even suspected that the government was preparing a plan to save the Island, a plan that was first referred to by its codename of Operation Violet, and which, having secretly received (also at first) its true logo of CONSTAT, ended up taking the definitive name of 'The Final Measure'. We, at least, know the complete text of the decree extracted from the plan. We lack knowledge of the text of its rules, but they were contained in the separate items of the plan anyway and needed only the indispensable adjustment of content to the technical norms of legislative editing to become regulatory. After all, it was a question of law.

The new meeting, which would also be the last of the four sessions of that day, was strictly secret in nature, the office totally sealed off. As had been done in previous meetings, besides turning on the red warning light above the three doors leading to the office, the General Co-ordinator personally locked them; in this case, the red light served only to indicate that there were people in the office since, if the doors had been simply locked for the three consecutive hours allotted to the development of the regulations, it could have induced someone into thinking—erroneously—that there was no one working in the office, when the contrary was the case: they were working, and diligently.

There was still one more additional step that could be taken to seal off the office. On the intercom, the General Director ordered an invisible secretary to hold all telephone calls—unless it was a personal call from the Director. SUPERCAP didn't want to be bothered during the allotted three consecutive hours since they would be entirely absorbed in the work of the decree's regulation. A refrigerator, duly stocked with water, drinks and fruit, was quickly brought into the office to forestall any thirst or hunger experienced by SUPERCAP's members. Thermos-flasks and cups were also provided with the same diligent, practical zeal: it wouldn't be for lack of coffee that the advisors managed without a strong stimulant to maintain open, alert productivity. However, since the waiters were also barred access to the office the advisors had to serve themselves. It must be said that these last touches, while they did not follow a deliberate psychological strategy planned by the General Co-ordinator, did have extraordinarily positive psychological effects on the advisors. Actually, the improvised arrangements for food and drink gave them an unexpected feeling of well-being, an agreeable intimacy very similar to that type of ingenuous, simple happiness which comes from doing work in the seclusion of one's home, in the back room, near the kitchen.

They prepared themselves to attack the regulations.

However, when the session opened, CLAN's President did raise a point of order.

'Although the matter has been termed to be of urgent priority, I think it will be impossible to develop the total regulatory body of the decree in the space of three hours.'

'But that is the time period which I led the Director to expect,' objected the General Co-ordinator, firmly. 'Let me be more specific since I fear that my esteemed colleague may not have sufficiently evaluated the degree of responsibility assumed by myself and, by extension, by all this council when I informed the Director that the regulations would be completed within the stipulated time frame. I told the

Director that the regulations would be concluded within three hours, is that understood? In three hours. No more than that: three hours. That's what I told the Director. And he naturally believes that in three hours the rules will have been delineated. And, knowing this, it's logical that he will be expecting to receive the regulations in three hours. That means: in three hours I will have to take the regulations, duly concluded, to the Director, in his office. Then, if this meeting was called with the express and sole purpose of developing these regulations, that means that once ended, that is, in three hours, in accordance with our work timetable, the regulations should be ready for me to take them up to the Director. I think that I have been sufficiently clear in presenting the information to my esteemed advisor.'

Inflexible, the other insisted.

'The time is too short for such extensive material. In the interest of the regulations themselves, of adequately explaining them, the Director must understand that the fabric of the rules will be inevitably compromised, failing in that which it aspires to be and should be: the totally detailed mechanism of the decree.'

'But I set the time,' said the General Co-ordinator. 'And, from the moment in which I set it, it became a stipulated period, or rather, a formally assumed responsibility operating in function of a predetermined time.'

'In that case, nothing easier,' said CLAN's president. 'When a time period is established to complete a certain thing, and that thing becomes impossible to do within the given deadline, the time period itself contains, inherently, the mechanism necessary to complete that thing within the time required for it. I am referring to the mechanism of renewal. After all, if renewal of a time period is a valid, acceptable recourse, this means that every deadline is renewable, in so far as there cannot be time renewal without first having stipulated the time period. Then, if there is a stipulated time, we have, consequently, the element indispensable to its renewal, which is, naturally, the span itself. The important thing is that the renewal results from the proven futility of doing something within a time period when that thing can only be done if the time period is extended. And this is exactly what is occurring with the regulations. It is absolutely impossible to do it within three hours.'

'That is, you are still insisting on the thesis of renewal?' asked the General Co-ordinator.

'Obviously,' responded the other.

The General Co-ordinator thought for a moment. And, after having considered, he suddenly changed his tactics, switching to arguments which, in his brief but fertile reflection, seemed to be more likely to overcome the resistance of CLAN's President and, at the same time, to win over the rest of the assembly. Would that it convinced his esteemed advisor! The work on the regulations was, by nature, minimal. There was no need for the advisors to submit themselves to new, lengthy planning sessions because, with respect to the polishing of ideas and to the ample, exhaustive debate undertaken to diagnose the problem and establish alternatives to the solution, the bulk of the work had already been defined in terms of an accomplished fact during the course of structuring the plan. And the plan had been approved! Thus, during this phase of work, all that the illustrious members of CLAN had to do was to equate the content of the plan with legislative norms from which plan a decree is extracted, and a decree's regulations are based on the plan which engendered it in so far as no plan can lack the formal expression tantamount to its conversion into a formal, legal instrument, in the total apparatus of the decree and the regulations which govern it. This is the same as saying that CLAN, in order to carry out the work of regulation, would only have to adjust the plan's proclaimed measures to the decree, thus regulating the decree and at the same time any material which, incapable of regulation in the plan might be presented in the plan for regulation in function of the decree. In other words: CLAN had only to give legislative editing to material which, although not legislatively edited, was basically edited. And to have the material basically edited (as the advisors well knew), was to have half the work done for whomever had to edit its regulations, since no regulation could regulate anything unless it basically existed as a function of the work one intended to develop with it as its base. Actually, it was only a question of converting the plan's content into articles, paragraphs and subheadings, systematizing it, codifying it, giving it, in sum, the incisive, serious tone of legislative editing—and CLAN, with its superior competence and the recognized authority of its presiding advisor, could finish the work perfectly within the stipulated time.

At this point, CLAN's President, who had been attentively accompanying the General Co-ordinator's argument, suddenly adopted an air of conclusive meditation: evidently, some idea had occurred to him.

The General Co-ordinator finished.

'Anyway, SCAN is on duty, waiting for the duly regulated decree in order to begin broadcasting tomorrow at 8 am via all forms of mass communication in order to achieve total informative coverage. The Director knows this, realizes this, and hopes for nothing else.'

And then CLAN's President, who really did have an idea, tried to say so to the General Co-ordinator. As he began to do so, one thing became very clear: although he didn't immediately say what his idea was, one could readily see that, giving in finally to the superior reasons invoked by the General Co-ordinator, he was disposed to reconsider, via the idea, his radical point of view in relation to the futility of regulating the decree within the time fixed.

'Bearing in mind the brevity of the time period, I see only one solution,' said CLAN's President.

All eyes were fixed on him. Oh, there was a solution! But, what could it be? A solution? This was very important, considering the brevity of the time. This meant that in spite of the brevity of the time, there was a solution? Without a doubt, this was truly extraordinary. However, it became indispensable to know how CLAN's President, after insisting that there was no way to make the time compatible with the regulation, managed to find a solution to make them compatible. And everyone wanted to know just what the solution was that the President of CLAN, 'bearing in mind the brevity of the time period', had found to the problem created by the deadline in relation to the work of regulation, without, obviously, thinking about renewing the term.

He met the assembly's general curiosity.

'As you all know, time is a problem. However, in view of the substantial arguments which our illustrous General Co-ordinator has just presented to this assemblage, it becomes imperative that we find a solution to the problem of the deadline. As I said before, the most natural solution would be to renew the term. But, since the measure to renew the time is impossible given the current circumstances and the urgency of finding a solution required by the problem, it is clear that we must seek a solution to the problem within the brief time period itself.'

'Very good,' said the General Co-ordinator.

'And the search for this solution,' continued CLAN's President, 'will have to be made in the sense of changing the conventional legislative structure, without prejudice to the law's support, by introducing intercomplementary co-ordinated data into the mechanism for the decree's regulation, as a function of a logical legislative deduction. In other words: we must divide the regulations in two distinct parts which are nonetheless complementary, both of which conform to the decree and together with it form a whole. Thus, bearing in mind the brevity of the term, I really only see one solution: develop a basic regulatory policy within the stipulated time, to be published along with the decree; and, later, complementary regulations to be developed during the space of four days. Outside of this, there is no solution.'

'But, we need to know if the Director will accept this solution,' pondered the General Co-ordinator. After all, what has been established is that I will take the regulations to him inside of three hours. It's only natural that he expect to receive the total ruling, not one in parts. Regulations in parts are an unedited fact according to technocratic legislation. I don't know how he will take the proposed solution.'

'In that case, there is only one solution,' said the CLAN's President.

'One solution?' wondered the General Co-ordinator. 'By chance, do you have another solution to offer?'

'Yes, in a way. The solution that I have to present is that the solution I presented be submitted to the decision of the Director. After all, if the problem is knowing whether or not he will accept the solution I suggested, then the only way our illustrious General Co-ordinator can know this is by submitting the solution for the Director's supreme consideration. In a word, the solution is to take the solution to the Director.'

The other nodded his head with decision.

'I'll do it. I would have to do it anyway. Meanwhile, for my own information, I'll ask the noble advisor to explain what the basic regulations consist of, and, naturally, what the complementary regulations are.'

'I consider this to be of extreme interest to us all,' interrupted the technician in organizational norms. 'I, in particular because of my speciality, am very curious to know just how the basic and complementary regulations would be organizationally defined, even if in general terms.'

'It's very simple,' answered the President of CLAN. 'The basic regulations involve the decree's immediate effects, while the complementary regulations involve forthcoming ones.'

'What do you mean by immediate effects?' asked the General Co-ordinator.

'I mean what should be understood as such. That is: the obligatory use of the pill, discounting the pill off of salaries, testimony propagandizing the use of the pill, and, naturally, punishment for those who break the contraception law. Above all, the means of execution by which transgressors will be punished will have to be written into the basic regulations.'

'And the forthcoming effects?' inquired the General Co-ordinator.

'The forthcoming effects are exactly those which will complement the immediate effects in the complex of measures to be adopted for the total implementation of the law. For example: fiscal incentives given to the pharmaceutical industry to increase production of the pill. Or, to cite another example, the gradual decrease in pregnancies

121

until their complete extinction. Anyway, both the immediate effects as well as the forthcoming effects are foreseen by the plan. All that remains for us to do is to order them, divide them up, and place them in the respective categories of the regulations, ranked according to degree of urgency, in so far as there will be a degree of immediate urgency and, similarly, a degree of forthcoming urgency.'

Following these last words by CLAN's President, SUPERCAP's members were silent for a minute while they looked at each other, with approving nods of their heads. The General Co-ordinator finally spoke.

'Well, since it is a question of material which depends on prior consultation with the Director, I will not submit it to the assembly. Actually, the assembly is not in a position to deliberate about material which can only be considered after the Director has recognized its validity as such. Without this, it cannot be considered to be material. Consequently, not yet being an item, it cannot be a particular on the agenda of our work. After all, it is a matter which, in its attempt to alter the regulations' structure and the established deadline, proposes the division of the regulations that the Director expects to receive as a whole within the sole, stipulated time period, which, in its turn, will also be divided in two by the material, implementing the time period of three hours with that of four days.'

He paused, and then decided.

'In view of the matter, let us suspend our work until I return from the Director's office; I will transmit his decision to you for the necessary and corresponding action.'

He got up, left the room, and went to give the material to the Director.

In his absence the advisors ate sandwiches, got drinks, and sipped coffee—after all, the work was suspended and they had to use the interval to do what it is that people do during breaks that pop up at meetings. And, as was natural, they also used the time to converse informally about the material under formal discussion before the break.

'There is no other solution than the one I presented,' CLAN's President never tired of repeating. 'Either we divide the regulations and, with it, the time, or we keep the stipulated deadline and don't finish the regulations. It cannot be done within the stated time frame.'

Finally, suddenly, in less time than was to be expected, the General Co-ordinator returned to the room. He had a smile on his face—a rare thing for him. However, without abdicating his dignity, he silently walked to the head of the table, and waited there in silence until he saw that all the advisors were seated in their respective places. Then, breaking the silence which hung over SUPERCAP and its members, he made his announcement.

'The Director has approved the division of the regulations. I want you also to know that I obtained the Director's permission to extend by one hour and forty-five minutes, the time we spent debating the proposal made by CLAN's esteemed President. Thus, the three hour time limit initially set for the regulations will begin at this time.'

A loud round of applause greeted his words, leaving him somewhat embarrassed. But, however emotional he was in view of SUPERCAP's spontaneous demonstration of appreciation for his victorious meeting with the Director, he knew how to control himself. And with an admirable sense of practicality and a no less admirable awareness of his responsibilities, instead of thanking them for their applause, he turned to the assemblage and spoke in a vigorous tone of command, quieting the euphoric handclapping.

'To work! There's no time to waste! Let's try to write the basic regulations without wasting more time! To work, Mr advisors, to work!'

Quickly, CLAN's members attacked the work of the basic regulations, based on what was already foreseen and approved in the plan. As for the rest of the advisors, now exempt from the responsibilities of structuring the plan, exhaustively developed under the combined efforts of all the assembly, based on a strong series of ideas and assistance— they were merely a part of the assembly now. But although secondary in appearance, this complementary work did not reduce the importance of their participation in the work of designing the basic regulations. After all, without the presence of the assembly, the basic regulations developed by CLAN could not be approved at SUPERCAP's level. Thus, perfectly aware of the urgency of their work, from that moment on, in one form or another, none of the advisors did anything else except work to finish the basic regulations within the three hours.

Seventeen

In two hours and 16 minutes of work, duly timed by the General Co-ordinator (after all, it was a non-renewable deadline), the basic regulations were ready, approved by the assembly without discussion because there was nothing to discuss—except for the item about the means of execution to be employed in the punishment, which was the object of divergent opinons before it was unanimously approved. (Later on we'll see what the measure was that was finally adopted.) Anyway, with the exception of this item, everything had been foreseen by the plan, and to it and to what was to constitute the basic regulations CLAN had only to give the legislative editing indispensible to the legal formalization of the items which, extracted from the plan, would be integrated into the basic body of the regulations as sections and paragraphs publicized with the decree.

'The first part of the regulations work is complete,' announced CLAN's President after the assembly had approved the final item.

'Would you be so kind as to proceed to the reading of the approved legal text,' said the General Co-ordinator.

'Art. I—To comply fully with the precepts of the Decree designated 'The Final Measure', and as a normative support for its principle objective, the obligatory use of the contraceptive pill will be instituted throughout the Island.

Subsection—Regardless of age and/or state of virginity, use of the pill will be obligatory for all women from their first menstrual cycle forward.

Art. II—All firms engaged in any type of industrial or commercial activity, and having 20 or more women employed during their regular work shifts, are hereby authorized to provide the women with the quantity of pills necessary for per capita consumption, to be deducted monthly from their salary. This authorization is also extended to those firms which, either independently or communally organized, are engaged in agricultural activities and employ 20 or more female workers, excluding those who work under contract as day labourers or piecework employees.

Subsection—Distribution of the pill in accord with the practices established under this article will follow strict price controls. Any improper increase in the price of the pill will result in a fine equivalent to the employee's salary of three months, levied against the distributor.

Art. III—For those women who break the legal precepts not subject to appeal, the death sentence mandated by the decree will be carried out by the executory authority's summary order, independent of due process.

Subsection—The only means of execution to be employed in the punishment will be one revolver shot to the heart. Under no circumstances will any other method have legal validity.

Art. IV—The following two acts constitute proof of violation of said law:

(a) medical/hospital verification of pregnancy of more than four months;

(b) bearing a child while the Decree is in effect.

Paragraph 1—In the case of violations of letter (B), punishment will be extended to the child, considered to be a criminal object as a natural consequence of the crime.

Paragraph 2—The validity of birth licences issued before the Decree's implementation is hereby guaranteed, said licences to be presented whenever the authorities so request.

Paragraph 3—Beginning with the Decree's date of publication, and as a consequence of its content, no more birth licences will be issued.

Art. V—The mandatory abortion law will remain in effect; unplanned abortions will also be permitted to avoid violations of the law as outlined in (a) and (b) of Article IV.'

Concluding his reading, the co-ordinator of CLAN turned to the General Co-ordinator.

'I was careful to write it in understandable language. How-

126

ever, due to the large number of revisions, perhaps it would be better to draft a final copy before our distinguished General Co-ordinator submits it to His Excellency, the Director.'

The General Co-ordinator asked for the text of the basic regulations which covered a little more than two and one half pages. With a vigilant stare of evaluation he scrutinized it from beginning to end.

'Yes . . . Without a doubt, the text is perfectly readable, although much amended. But, given the urgency of the case, His Excellency, the Director, will know how to overlook the confusion in certain paragraphs. I'll take the text as it is to the Director. After all, the deadline is approaching. There is no time to lose.'

And worried about not losing any time, he tried to save some, hurriedly leaving the room to take the manuscript to the Director. And, just as quickly as he left, he returned, which made the assembly think that the Director, also preoccupied with the deadline, had read the text of the basic regulations as rapidly as possible. Anyway, spurred on by time, the General Co-ordinator and the Director himself had both rid themselves of their work in a race against time.

But while they hadn't perceived it in the first instant of the General Co-ordinator's unexpected return, the advisors suddenly, and with undisguised surprise, realized that he didn't have anything in his hand. A momentary doubt assaulted them. What about the text? Could His Excellency, the Director, still be reading it? Or, simply, hadn't he approved it? If that was the case, what about the deadline?

None of the above had happened.

And, before they had a chance to sit down—thus breaking in an unexpected manner, the strictness of his habits of protocol—the General Co-ordinator clarified.

'His Excellency, the Director, approved the text as it stands. To save time, I stopped off at the Mecanographics section and left the manuscript with the head of the department. In 20 minutes the text will be typed up. Which means that the Director will be able to sign the basic regulations within the time frame that he so justly wanted.'

He sat down.

'I would like to express my thanks to all of you gentlemen, and particularly, to the members of CLAN, represented by the presence of its illustrious President, for the productive efforts put forth to develop the basic regulations, without which this important document could not have been ready in time for typing and signing before the deadline.'

He paused, consulting his statement.

'With these thanks, which you well deserve, I now declare the meeting adjourned, and call the next session for tomorrow at nine o'clock, to develop the supplementary regulations.'

He arose, and with him, all the assembly, which quickly dispersed in search of a well-earned domestic rest. The advisors, however, didn't really get a chance to rest—at least, while they were awake. A strong feeling of expectation, of gnawing anxiety, of unsatisfied speculation—in short: a vague and generalized fear that perhaps they had done something wrong induced them to believe that they would only rest after hearing the radio and reading the papers tomorrow morning.

Eighteen

At 7.00 am, as per the broadcast plan developed and carried out by SCAN, The Final Measure was announced to the whole Island Population. Every half hour, the radio would broadcast (on tape) the text of the decree and its basic regulations. The systematic and rigorously timed repetition of the transmission, preceded by a strident drum roll, obeyed a strategy the mass communication technicians had recommended to the radio transmission services as part of the Total Plan for Mass Information with Repetitive Extension. (That's what the technicians called the plan.) Gathered around the radio, listening to what they had prepared for others to hear, the advisors felt a kind of twisted emotion like a feeling of perplexed complicity, which they repressed and disguised, taking refuge in a progressive torpor of spirit from which came, along with the consolation of duty carried out, the certainty that—finally—they could really rest: the text had arrived on time at SCAN.

And as they dressed, they spent (including breakfast) a minimum amount of time in getting ready, since at 9.00 am they had to be at the first meeting for the development of the supplementary regulations, to be concluded and presented, as we all know, within the nonrenewable time perid of four days. CLAN's own co-ordinator had asked for this time frame and there was no reason now not to comply with it. But we're not going to talk of that now. What we're going to talk about now is what happened on the Island during the four days in which SUPERCAP met to consider the supplementary regulations which, once the deadline was up, were duly announced to the Island population, as later on they will be to the reader.

Actually, after the morning transmissions repeated every half hour (on tape), the Total Plan for Mass Information with Repetitive Extension permitted the total Island population to take gradual note of the new law without the slightest risk of information distortion, so common with second-hand news spread from person to person. Whoever didn't turn on his radio early in the morning could turn it on whenever they wanted and the notice, emanating from its authorized source, would reach his ears. Between announcements, dance music was played. No songs, because the technicians thought that singing was a diversionary auditory element capable of reducing the impact of the news. The recommendation was restrictive: under no circumstances would any words be broadcast that did not have to do with the text of the notice. This limitation, naturally, extended to the words of songs. Thus, the instrumental dance numbers, duly purged of words, were interspersed with announcements to the listeners, broadcast in the form of alerts: 'Attention! Attention! Keep your radios tuned to this station! In a few minutes, we will broadcast an announcement of extreme importance to all the Island!' And, as promised, one had only to wait a few minutes and the news would be repeatedly transmitted.

In case of reception failure, interference from some domestic noise, possible lack of immediate comprehension, or even of an occasional distraction (after all, a stray thought could cause a possible distraction while a person was listening to the news), the listener had the option of paying closer attention while again listening to the news, invariably repeatedly as before. Also, if upon first impact of hearing the news, a person should say to himself in true and sincere but perfectly understandable shock: 'It's not possible! I must have misunderstood . . .', one had only to listen again, as many times as necessary, since, after a time, with so many repetitions, there was no one incredulous or stupid enough not to believe that what they had heard was really what was said.

Anyway, suppose in a casual meeting on the street or during a gossipy phone call, someone were to say,

'Did you hear the latest? The government has just passed a new law against the population explosion. I just heard it on the radio.'

And, with busybody agitation, he would pass on (in detail) the news which coincidentally the other had not yet heard; that other person could, for his part, easily confirm the news by turning on the radio (in some cases, the car radio), or by running to the nearest bar with the satisfied assurance that where there was a bar, there had to be a radio turned on. Then, even if he did have to contain his curiosity for a minute or so while listening to one or two instrumental dance numbers, in hopes of catching the broadcast during one of the news breaks—with the announcer's repeated bulletins, he could quickly confirm that the person who told him the news had neither exaggerated nor made it up.

The advantages of 'repetitive extension'.

Besides, when the mass communication technicians had developed the Total Plan for Mass Information with Repetitive Extension (TOPMIRE) to broadcast 'The Final Measure' decree and its regulations, they had given the plan a 'repetitive extension' exactly because they had thought that the repetitive extension would bring only advantages to the news broadcast, or—to use their words—to the 'operations of information', in so far as, functioning as a provision of the systematic reiteration of the news, the 'repetive extension' would assurè that the more repetitions of the broadcast there were, the larger the audience would be.

'It is necessary to repeat the notice, repeat it systematically, in order to avoid having the news, because of lack of repetition, turn into antinews, disinforming instead of informing,' emphasized one of the technicians during the debate over TOPMIRE's evaluation.

'Perfect!' agreed a second technician. 'Antinews dis-serves information as it dis-serves the notice itself, because, antinews being the contrary to the news, it distorts and falsifies the true announcement, bringing the news down to the rumour level. Thus, as the antinews is only possible when lack of information gives it life, one must recognize that the only means of stopping the course of the antinews is to retroactively feed the information to the people by systematically repeating the notice.'

'Perfect!' agreed a third technician. 'The systematic

repetition of the news is the only means of preserving its integrity. Besides, in developing the Total Plan for Mass Information with Repetitive Extension to broadcast 'The Final Measure' decree, we had no other objective in mind when we adopted this strategy of reiteration other than that of preserving the text of the decree and its regulations in their entirety, so that later no one could say that they had not followed the decree's orders because they had not understood them well, or because they had only understood them in part because someone had mentioned them in passing, or simply because they hadn't heard of the law's existence. Actually, this will never happen. And it will not happen because, while TOPMIRE's 'repetitive extension' functions as a mechanism of the news' systematic repetition, this mechanism will not only broadcast the notice but, above all, establish a means of permanent verification. And, because of its systematic repetition, from the moment in which the news is established at a level of permanent verification, this will mean that the notice, in so far as it becomes permanently verified, will be safeguarded in its entirety, within the reach of each and every individual.

'Perfect!' cried the first technician in agreement.

Finally, after the Total Plan for Mass Information with Repetitive Extension had been evaluated, the mass communications technicians, who had developed it with the specific objective of universally informing the Island's population, agreed that the Island's population would really only be totally informed when every individual had access to the information. Thus, as the coverage of this goal of informative reciprocity, objectifying the individual/mass relationship, had been previously assured thanks to the 'repetitive extension' mechanism—they concluded their evaluation of the Plan, repeating to one another,

'Perfect. Perfect. Perfect.'

And since everything was perfect, the Total Plan for Mass Information with Repetitive Extension was begun the morning of the next day, in stages of converging actions, according to a strategy recommended by the technicians who had developed it. The first of these actions, as we have seen, took place at 7.00 am, on network radio, with the systematic broadcast (every half hour) of the decree's text and basic regulations. The second action was initiated through the newspapers which began to circulate at 9.00 am with an obvious, but expected, delay. You see, between 5.00 and 7.00 am, SCAN had been careful to announce to the public, every 15 minutes, over the radio, that on that day the newspapers would follow a special publication schedule with a three hour delay. (They usually came out at 6.00 am). This meant that in the intervening two hours (from 5.00 to 7.00 am) SCAN's announcement would be on the air eight times, without, however, going into the reasons behind the delay. The motives for the delay were not explained, nor did SCAN, in utilizing the broadcast expedient, think about explaining anything to the public, being careful only to warn them, with chronometric, informative zeal, that the newspapers would come out three hours late that day. In addition, there was the spontaneous collaboration of the newsboys who, stationed patiently at the stands, patiently took on the responsibility of informing the public that the newspapers had not yet come out—but that they soon would. The newspaper boys had been previously informed of the delay by UNISEND (Unified Services for Newspaper Delivery). Thus, while they waited for delivery, they were careful to pass on the information to any persons who, not having had on the radio during SCAN's broadcast of the announcement, strolled up to buy a newspaper at their customary hour.

Finally, at 9.00 am, UNISEND's vans began to deliver the newspapers to the stands. And, in the flurry of distribution, as the delivery boys in their banana-yellow overalls dumped off the bundles of papers at the stands, they gave the newsboys their own versions of the delay.

'They doubled the circulation today and even made a special edition. If they don't break even, pal, we're going to be reading in the afternoons only.'

Since the number of issues was doubled, the circulation naturally was doubled, too, as was that of the sales, just as SCAN had foreseen when they established the relationship between the informative interest of the material *vis-à-vis* the reader as reader, and consumer interest in the material *vis-à-vis* the reader as buyer—that is: the relation between the interests of consumption of the material as a function of the material, and the interest of the material as a function of consumption. And when the public, attracted by the banner headlines announcing 'The Final Measure', threw themselves into buying the papers with avid curiosity, they realized that such serious material, along with the evident toil involved in its preparation, justified in itself the delay in the papers' publication—independent of the extra time that the newspaper offices, on overtime, had to put in to get the newspapers on the streets with double circulation.

Although the headlines varied, 'The Final Measure' was invariably mentioned in them as the principle informational-graphic component for the communicative message. In this sense, SCAN had recommended to the layout artists that the title of the decree stand out on the front page headlines, not only to enhance its status as informational nexus for the graphic cluster, but also to assure the multivalent effect of a visual-mnemonic reminder within the information context: once seen, it would never be forgotten, nor would it be forgotten after it was seen. A simple problem of reciprocal stimulus. After all, the insistent, systematic reference to the decree in the newspaper headlines had a subjective intention transcending the layout's strategy, although it did utilize it in order to achieve that which SCAN's technicians considered to be the persuasive goal of the information. The intention—subjective—was the following: associate the name of the decree in such a manner with the idea of a single, redeeming act of providence that it would acquire the epic dimension of collective legend, and, at the same time, symbolize the feelings of a people unified behind one will and one objective: combating at any price the population explosion in order to survive. (With regard to this unification, SCAN's technicians had no doubts, since the Island population would have only one option if they reacted against this decree: die of hunger.)

And there were the headlines on the front pages of the newspapers, laid out according to the objective and subjective effects foreseen by SCAN:

GOVERNMENT DECREES FINAL MEASURE
TO SAVE ISLAND POPULATION FROM
STARVATION

THE FINAL MEASURE IS THE SOLUTION
TO AVOID DEATH BY STARVATION

DEATH BY STARVATION WILL BE AVOIDED
BY THE FINAL MEASURE

And, attracted by the headlines, everyone bought papers. After all, the headlines announced that the government had found a solution—'The Final Measure'—to save the Island population from the sombre end which threatened it: death by starvation.

Thus, between the fear of increasing food shortages and the panic about the demographic explosion, with hunger stalking the people and the government stepping in in time to banish it, routing it out with a vigorous, saving measure—the papers were sold out in a little more than two hours in spite of the double edition.

As a footnote, also on the first pages, the following important recommendation was made to the reader: 'Cut out the text of "The Final Measure" decree with its basic regulations. You stand only to gain by it. In case of doubt, consult your copy without delay.' When it decided to include the footnote, SCAN kept in mind that 'poor or late comprehension of the decree's text will inevitably be prejudicial to the interactive relationship between the government and members of the community.' Besides, and still according to the technicians of SCAN, 'no interaction is possible without correspondence between a governmental communication and a fully, effectively, informed community'.

At 11.00 am the third of the 'convergent actions' took place. It was television's turn. The regular TV broadcast schedule began at that hour and continued until midnight. During those four days, however, it followed the Saturday programming schedule which added two extra hours to the regular programming. The interest in adapting the 'repetitive extention' to television, giving the mass information plan an audiovisual coverage of higher schedule yield, led the technicians to include this exceptional measure in TOP-MIRE. Thus, although it was an exceptional measure, it did conform to the limits of scheduled exceptionality since, by adopting as an exceptional measure the Saturday schedule for TOPMIRE's four planned days of mass communication via TV, they were careful to avoid having the exceptional augmentation of the regular TV programming schedule overstep the four days of Saturday exceptional scheduling.

We've already said (but we'll remind you here one more time) that the Island had only one TV station which, together with two radio stations and three newspapers, formed the State Complex of Amalgamated News, i.e., the abbreviated SCAN, so often referred to in this chapter. The broadcasts began with the programme entitled 'The Eleven O'clock News', for obvious chronometrical reasons. (After all, the broadcasts did begin at 11.00.)

On that day, The Eleven O'clock News was entirely dedicated to 'The Final Measure', with two anchormen first reading the text of the decree and its basic regulations in dynamic alternation, then, in a lively sequence of images, various shots of SUPERCAP's opening session were shown (on film) with a cut to the Director's office, documenting the historic moment in which he signed the decree. The narrator's voice described the events in the documentary. Finally, captured panoramically, orchestrally backed, a rich, waving field of grain was shown on the screen, suggesting a bucolic harvest of plenty—the government's message was read contrasting the threat of starvation with the infallible perspective of an abundant future, based on the prognosis of the decree's effects.

And the News closed without the annoyance of commercial interruptions since Island TV, serving the administration's high interests, had as the only sponsor for its programming the government, which haughtily rejected the commercial degradation of selling time, thus prohibiting such an important mass communication vehicle from carrying to the masses, sandwiched between an announcement of public interest made without cost to the public, a utilitarian message of interest to the advertiser with its inevitable onus on the public. Anyway, the just and necessary informing of the public, which the government safeguarded with such care and zeal, could not suffer the discontinuity of intermittent and astute commerical interruptions—exactly because the government, making TV the official vehicle for the administration's voice, had to bring the purified and exclusive word of the government to the masses cleanly, with pure and official integrity.

'The Eleven O'clock News' was regularly and habitually followed by the other news shows—the 2.00, 5.00, 8.00 and finally, the 11.00 news. On Saturdays, with the extended exceptional programming time, the principle events of the preceding week were recapped on the programme 'Information Synthesis', broadcast in the first quarter hour after 12.30 am—an extra, brief spot befitting a synthesis. Afterwards came the closing newsreel which opened the first two sleepless hours of Sunday and closed Saturday's programming. The next day, to begin again TV's broadcasting, the 'Eleven O'clock News' returned, to be followed by the others with scheduled and programmed punctuality, in recurring and attentive efforts to bring new news. On that day, however, as part of TOPMIRE's repetitive scheme for TV, the 'Eleven O'clock News' returned repeatedly during the different hours of the other news shows, repeating at 2, 5, 8 and 11 all that it had said about 'The Final Measure' at 11.00 am. And, as it exceptionally followed the Saturday schedule, it also occupied the time slot of Informative Synthesis which, renouncing its objectives of summarizing and synthesizing, repeated the news in its entirety. The previous tape of the 'Eleven O'clock News' was an effective means for its exact reproduction on all the news shows, including the Saturday Synthesis show, exceptionally programmed for Tuesday through Friday during the four days in which 'The Final Measure' would be publicized as TOPMIRE had established.

During the unusual adoption of the Saturday schedule, the programme was run in its entirety, with the customary newsreel finish on the next day. TOPMIRE's technicians had not abandoned the ideal of the film. The reasons for this were: if, during the Saturday programming context, the film constituted a complementary item to the schedule/programme, evidently, the Saturday programming, adopted in its total schedule, could only be considered as such, in terms of scheduled coverage, if the film was included to complement the schedule/programme and close the daily programming schedule.

However, one of the technicians added a subtle yet practical reason to the formal ones for showing the film: the film acted as leisure support, capable of positively contributing to the easing of eventual tensions produced by the decree on the spirits of the viewers as persons psychologically isolated, although possessing interpersonal relations directed toward a state of communal spirit. The important thing was that the film be carefully selected: no stories about babies.

Finally, when the TV coverage was finished, the 'convergent actions' strategy was completed, based on TOP-MIRE's fundamental items, with the graduated operational support of SCAN's communications mechanism. Everything was perfect. Grouped in a scheme of tripart conveyance, the mass communication vehicles—radio, press, television—exercised their converging actions to communicate the decree to the Island community, fulfilling TOPMIRE's time table, and doing so with such converging efficiency that already on the first day, without any other announcements on the radio, without having read any other announcement in the papers, and without any other notices on the 'News' shows, all the Island community was duly informed of that which, in their own interests and in harmony with the high interests of government, was their mass duty to understand: the text of 'The Final Measure' and its basic regulations.

Teodorico, as did everyone else, heard the radio on that day. Like everyone else, he read the newspapers. As did everyone else, he heard/saw the news on the television although he didn't have a set, but then neither did everyone else—but his neighbour had one, and it was no time to stand on ceremony. Come in, sit down, watch the programme. The welcome was explainable: between neighbours there was a kind of uncontrolled communicative impulse to meet, a kind of community necessity to share in the communication act which, as TOPMIRE's technicians had foreseen in their prognosis audience, produced 'a cordial, receptive identity between the TV user and the collective destination of the message transmitted via TV'—anyway, it explained the presence of the neighbour who didn't have a TV in the house of one who did.

Teodorico figured in TOPMIRE's 'teleaudience prognosis'. Thus, after hearing the text of the decree and its basic regulations on the radio and reading about it in the newspaper (actually, he read all three) he listened to it one more time on the penultimate 'News' show which, beside offering him the chance to hear it once again for repetitive confirmation, had the extra-auditory advantage of seeing the broadcast live, with photos efficiently illustrating SUPERCAP's meeting, and being able to see—with the vague joy of privileged indiscretion—the Director sign the decree in his office.

He returned home entirely informed and consoled. His consolation was the product of a pleasant, arithmetical and official confirmation: if after the initiation of the decree, no woman could have children for 40 years, his wife, who was already in an advanced state of legal pregnancy, could in four months have the awaited Teodorico Junior, the sum of those two, she and he, mother and father—legally acquired before the law went into effect. After all, even if he did understand more about shoes than he did about laws, our cobbler Teodorico, in the glow of paternity put into perspective, had learned enough about laws with the decree to know with comfort that the law is not retroactive.

On the second day, SCAN gradually reduced the number of broadcasts regarding the decree. TOPMIRE had recommended the reduction in broadcasts, as a function of a strategy of gradually increasing the intervals, which ended up having the effect of gradually increasing the interval between announcements about the decree while it gradually reduced the number of broadcasts on the radio. But with reason! The object was the following: to raise the effectiveness of the decree's publication which, if it were maintained at the original level of scheduled broadcasts, would suffer an inevitable communicative loss, with possible negative consequences for its effect on mass information. One of TOPMIRE's technicians offered an illuminating perspective on this matter: 'As long as the decree can only reach the masses via dissemination, the dissemination of the decree with gradually lose the public's interest as the masses learn about it. This means that, after being widely informed about the decree, the masses will reach a state of publication saturation, and the dissemination of the decree will no longer be of interest to them. Therefore it becomes necessary gradually to reduce the dissemination of the decree as the public becomes informed as to its contents, in order to adjust the interests of the decree's publication with those of informing the masses, who cannot suffer a decrease in interest during the four programmed days of mass information. In a certain sense, one could actually say that after the informative impact of the first day, the less access the public has to the decree, the more important the informative interest of the decree will be on subsequent days. Previous experience with mass information campaigns lead us to affirm that no information can be massively communicated without first having at least four days of gradual operation in dissemination. And this is because, in the process of universalizing a message, as in the case of the decree, the important thing is that the message, after its initial impact on the masses, not be maintained at a level of exhaustive dissemination which depletes broadcast interest, but rather it should be maintained at a level of measured dissemination, gradually reduced, and as it is reduced in length, it should be concentrated in its informative essence, which gives the message a residual permanent interest. Then, overcoming the conditioning of the dissemination, the message assumes an absolute value in and of itself, gradually embedding itself in the masses so that, once implanted, it finally becomes universal. Besides, without this embedding there can be no universalization; nothing becomes universal without first becoming embedded, and embedding something, in terms of information, is nothing more than—to take the example of universalizing the decree—the gradual worth enhancement of the effect of the information on the masses, not as a result of the dissemination, but of a whole process of informative sedimentation, of which dissemination as a vehicle of information is only one component. Actually, TOPMIRE recommends repetitive extension for the dissemination of the decree. This, however, does not invalidate the strategy of gradual reduction in dissemination, rather it justifies it. The announcements must be gradually reduced to the point at which the decree, because of its gradual implantation into the masses, will no longer need them. We should not forget that dissemination is only one stage in the process of universalization. And, above all, we cannot forget that the decree has an informative value which is inherent. Which means that the informative value of the decree is not the result of dissemination, but is its only and highest motive.'

The technician's perspective caused a vivid impression on the other members of TechTAF charged with developing TOPMIRE; they not only adopted and approved it, but also immediately established a scale of gradually reduced radio broadcasts for the decree, based on his presentation. Thus, on the second day, instead of being broadcast every half hour as had happened the first day, the decree was heard every 45 minutes. On the third day, a new reduction took place: the decree was heard every hour. Finally, on the fourth day, it was broadcast every two hours. After evaluating all the alternatives, this scale seemed to be the one which would most efficiently serve the decree's objectives of sedimentation and universalization within the stated time period.

The newspapers also adjusted their coverage to the strategy of gradually reduced dissemination. On the second day, the headlines referring to the decree were substituted by a caption at the bottom of the front page where the text of the decree, written in 14 point type, was published word for word with the following note: 'See the basic regulations of the decree on page 2.' On the third day, the caption gave way to a bold-faced arrow, asking the reader to turn to page 3 where, in two columns, he could read the text of the decree and its basic regulations. Finally, on the fourth day, without invalidating the dissemination's repetitive extension, the decree was transferred to page 4 where it appeared for the last time in the press with its basic regulations, while on the front page, footnoted, a long title comprehensively announced: 'Tomorrow the Supplementary Regulations to "The Final Measure" will be published.'

The TV, while it obeyed different techniques permitted it by its specific communication resources, was also careful to gradually reduce the decree's broadcasts, adopting a 'communicative system of interaction by alternation'. During one 'News' show (after the first one), two announcers (who also alternated turns) read the text of the decree without comment. On the next 'News' show, after a few brief comments about the decree's text in which were highlighted the timeliness and the extent of the measure taken by the government, from five to six, two announcers presented 'eye witness reports' from famous feminine personalities who were already using the pill. The first of these personalities to be interviewed was the Director's own wife—to set a good example, which in this case was the tonic to the interviews. After swallowing her daily contraceptive pill in front of the cameras, in the promise of a wholesome intimacy open to the feminine television viewing public, she declared, 'For three years I've been taking the pill daily and I'm only sorry that I didn't begin earlier. In these difficult times, I appeal to all the women on the Island to co-operate with the government's contraceptive campaign and take, as I do, the pill. Renouncing motherhood, more than an irreversible requirement of the law, is a question of conscience for all Island women, from whom the community expects the most dedicated and faithful observance of "The Final Measure". The population explosion is a threat to the Island's survival. In a word, it means hunger. To combat it, the government first needs the co-operation of each of us, of all of us. Let us unite, then, around the government to combat ceaselessly the population explosion by taking the pill. The law is with us. And we are with the law. Instead of children, pills. Instead of babies, more bread.'

Four more 'testimonials' from wives of high government officials followed, in order of the hierarchical importance of their husband's positions, with words that were not always the same, but which had the same objective: urge the women of the Island to use the life-saving pill which, after all, was the most practical form of saving themselves from starvation, and, at the same time, saving the Island from hunger. In consideration of her rank, the other interviewees avoided repeating the singularly personal gesture made by the First Lady by taking the pill in front of the cameras, although they did not forget to mention the daily use of the pill. In one form or another, they did not forget to mention the decree either, covertly insinuating to their viewers in their messages that between dying of hunger by not taking the pill, and being executed for breaking the law by not taking the pill, it was better to take the pill. After all, having babies, creating more people on the Island, is what was no longer possible.

The next 'News' show reproduced word for word the first 'News' show, with two announcers reading the text of the decree and its basic regulations. Next, new 'news' with 'live testimonials'. And thus, successively, in accord with the 'communicative system of interaction by alternation', the 'News' TV shows alternated during the four days, now transmitting the decree and its basic regulations (without comment), now airing (with brief comments prior to the decree) the 'testimonials' of high government authorities' wives, in decreasing order of importance. Only one point in this plan was altered, and the motive behind the alteration was due to the extraordinary effect on public opinion caused by the First Lady's deposition, or more precisely, by the final remarks contained in her spontaneous, yet edifying, statement: 'Instead of children, pills. Instead of babies, more bread.' The technicians of IVPO (Institute for the Verification of Public Opinion) registered a record number of points for this interview as compared with its model-interview, made with a standard viewing audience, in groups which SSOVPO (Sector for the Sampling of Opinions from the Verification of Public Opinion) indicated were standard-

collectivities: it was not necessary to interview anyone else. After all, the alteration to the plan, without prejudice to the informative accountability of the 'communicative system of interaction by alternation', consisted of the following: on the last 'News' shows of the fourth day (including the reading of the decree) they would rerun (on tape) the First Lady's 'testimonial'. After rerunning the 'testimonial' on the closing 'News' show, which also concluded TV's dissemination of 'The Final Measure' and its basic regulations, an announcer directed this short, polished message to the viewers, 'Your attention, please! Tomorrow, during regular programming hours, we will broadcast the supplementary regulations to "The Final Measure". Good night.'
night.'

Nineteen

During the four days programmed for the dissemination of the decree and its basic regulations, SUPERCAP met to prepare the supplementary regulations. While one regulation was announced, another was being prepared to complement the first, which in turn, complemented the decree, which, in turn, would be completely regulated in so far as one regulation complemented another. Meanwhile, working round the clock, SUPERCAP managed to complete their important task in two and a half days; the supplementary regulations were ready with a safety margin of one and a half days, although they were not publicized—as had been previously established, anyway—until the fourth day of dissemination of the decree and its basic regulations.

The dissemination of the supplementary rules obeyed a plan which was much simpler than that of the basic regulations. TOPMIRE classified it as an 'anti-extensive plan, of compacted communication'. This explains why, then, the dissemination of the supplementary regulations took only one day instead of four.

On the radio, in accord with the 'anti-extensive guided schedule' established by SCAN, based on the anti-extensive plan recommended by TOPMIRE, the text's dissemination was limited to ten compact announcements, spaced two hours apart, not to extend past midnight when, anti-extensively, the matter would be closed in terms of radio coverage.

The newspapers, with an absolutely customary circulation, dedicated the whole front page to its word for word publication, and from then on, did not print it on any other page, nor on any other day. The headlines stressed the fact that with the publication of the supplementary regulations the decree had been completely regulated, in order to avoid any doubts in this respect. After all, without this informative precaution, taken in the interests of properly informing the public, someone could uninformedly imagine that there was still something else to come, some item to be added to the decree. One cannot have much trust in the perceptive intelligence of the mass public.

For its part, TV dedicated all the 'News' shows of one day to the rules, with two announcers alternately reading the constituent items of the decree's important supplementary document—and that was all. For TV dissemination, no one thought of turning to the exceptionally long Saturday schedule even if it were of an exceptional nature, because, as an entity integrated into SCAN, TV had to integrate itself into the 'anti-extensive plan' of TOPMIRE, which SCAN had put into effect to disseminate the supplementary regulations.

After all, the supplementary regulations had little to do with the masses, so they were not universally publicized as the basic regulation had been when they came out with the decree. Let's clarify, though, that they had little to do with the masses in a direct manner; because, in an indirect manner, they did involve the masses in secondary effects, although the secondary nature of its effects were independent of the mass dissemination action. This was the opinion of TOP-MIRE's techno-narrator, who made the following observation: 'A problem is resolved by a solution after which said problem fundamentally ceases to exist. Fundamentally ceasing to exist, however, does not meant that other problems do not arise to take its place, as secondary effects of the very solution engendered by the problem. Actually, no problem can be resolved without producing, on the level of secondary effects, a series of residual problems which demand the adoption of parallel support measures destined to adjust the isolated solution of each new problem to the total solution of the problem. After all, as long as the residual problems, with their isolated solutions, contribute to modifying the original conditions which created the problem, they cannot change the fundamental solution in function of which the problem ceased to exist. This is what happens with the problem of the population explosion which fundamentally concerns us. A solution for it was found: "The Final Measure", in function of which the population explosion ceases to exist as a problem. In its place, other problems arise: the so-called residual problems which the solution to any problem produces in its major or minor secondary effects. I ask you: will these residual problems modify "The Final Measure" as a solution, even if their solutions modify the conditions which gave origin to the population explosion as a problem? Evidently not. "The Final Measure" will persist as a solution, since outside of it, there are no other solutions to the problem. Either we reduce the Island's population by "The Final Measure" to the point in which, within perfect conditions of survival, the demographic context is in harmony with the geographic area which contains it, or hunger will do away with the Island. And, in that case, instead of having a demographic context adjusted to the physical and vital reality of its geographic area, we will have, purely and simply, empty geographic space where the last man on the Island—without a job, without bread, without business—will die in the blackest misery, in a state of absolute solitude. Returning to the residual problems, I ask you: as a solution to the population explosion, what residual problems did "The Final Measure" cause by its secondary effects? The answer is simple: the residual problems it caused are linked directly to entities and institutions and, indirectly, to the community. As such, they were taken care of by the supplementary regulations to the decree which, complementing the basic regulations, from which they resulted as a cause of the decree, indicates the adequate solution through a series of supportive measures executed in the decree. What is important, then, for the masses in terms of the population explosion problem is the solution in function of which the population explosion will cease to exist, and not the supportive measures suggested by the residual problems with a view to overcoming the secondary effects of the decree. Which means, in sum, that what is important to the masses is the fundamental problem of the masses—that is: the population explosion which threatens them with starvation, and, naturally, its solution, which was communicated universally to the masses, anyway. Thus, in so far as the solution to the fundamental problem of the masses, contained in the decree and its basic regulations, was universally communicated to the masses, because it was of direct interest to them, the supplementary regulations of the decree, containing residual problems which do not directly interest the masses, do not require universal communication, the motive for which it will only be disseminated on an interest scale commensurate with its publicized goal: to the entities and institutions directly involved in it.'

In view of such irrefutable arguments, the dissemination of the supplementary regulations proceeded in the form we already know about.

And the residual problems?

Once the supplementary regulations were published, they were no longer hidden—including from the one telling this story. From the lips of the narrator, the reader will now know of them.

In the first place, the obligatory use of the pill, established by the decree, would lead to an appreciable elevation in the indexes of demand and consumption which routine production would not be able to meet. One new problem, therefore, but one which found a quick solution. Through the supplementary regulations, the government adopted a position compatible with the necessities of the product's industrial expansion, creating fiscal incentives destined to benefit production costs by augmenting the production of the pill. Result: the fiscal taxes incurred by the pharmaceutical industry, while maintained for other products in this area, aided the cost of producing the pill by reducing it 31.7 per cent, safeguarding the commercial price of the product which did not suffer any changes. If they had changed, there wouldn't have been any industrial benefits, and the production incentives would no longer be incentives. Logically, the laboratories which made pills began to make more of them—because, parallel to the reduction of taxes, the government established minimum obligatory levels of production for the pill which, in order to be adequately met,

148

required the laboratories to work on overtime as total levels of production rose. After all, if the minimum obligatory production levels were not met—there were fines. Which means that if the minimum obligatory level established for the pill's production created a new problem, a residual one—that problem was also resolved.

But the incentives didn't stop there. Toy factories were urged to convert their industrial facilities into laboratories to produce the pill, with generous official financial assistance, an interest rate which was practically symbolic, and a loan period of 11 years, prorated at $11\frac{1}{2}$. Deferred interest rates and a tax of one per cent would be charged during the extension, at the end of which, in case of eventual insolvency, the debt would be foreclosed, naturally. Nonetheless, the debtor would be free of any additional burdens except for the interest added to the principle during the moratorium. Strongly motivated, all the toy factories took advantage of the financing offered by the Industrial Conversion Credit Council, especially created to resolve—on the level of the decree's secondary effects—the problem of buying the equipment needed to manufacture the pill instead of toys. Besides, without children, there was no need for toys, since, in the last analysis, making toys would be a bad business risk just as making the pill because of its obligatory use, would be a good one. Naturally, SUPERCAP's technicians, men of solid technical-analytical backgrounds, endowed with a meticulous yet ample vision of problems and their corresponding and adequate solutions, would not forget that during the first years of the decree's implementation, there would be a residual percentage of children growing up, and it would be licit to admit that during this specific period of their lives, they would need toys. The evidence of this chronological fact, however, did not worry them to the point of judging it necessary to recommend to the government that there be some permissive tolerance granted in letting the toy manufacturers continue to make toys for a while. On the contrary, via their distributors, toy manufacturers were required to promote the liquidation of their stock, reduced 35 per cent in price, within the non-renewable time period of

149

30 days. Once the time for the liquidation of the stock was up, if any toys were left, the government would summarily confiscate them and distribute them for free during a 15 day nonsubscription lottery—and it was logical that with this measure, no toys would be left. Whatever the case, the essential thing was that within 45 days, counting the 15 of free distribution, the toy stock would be exhausted, since, in addition to the toys, in the interests of the government and the Island people and the toy manufacturers themselves—there was the pill. After all, it wasn't fair that by using the irrelevant, troublesome excuse of the stock stubbornly resisting liquidation, the toy manufacturers should slow down the fruition of the incentives and benefits offered by the government to get them to freely manufacture and sell the pill instead of toys (whose manufacture was prohibited, anyway).

But, if in cases of non-liquidation of stock within the prescribed time, the government was disposed to appropriating the toys and distributing them for free, would the public be so silly as to buy the toys when they could get them for free? Or were they so hungry for toys that they couldn't wait the 30 days for the free distribution? Now, it was obvious that free distribution carried out by non-subscription lottery would not permit one to choose the toys as when one buys them. But in any case, in order to safeguard the toy manufacturer's sale profit index, and above all, to make it perfectly clear that the government had no intentions of hurting the manufacturers by adopting the toy appropriation measure—SUPERCAP's technicians did not include the measure in the supplementary regulations. Maintained in strict secrecy, the appropriation measure, a part of common law, would only be publicized after the time period for the liquidation of the stock was up, and it was verified that toys were still on hand.

In spite of the extension of its consideration for play, it was evident that during the first years of the decree's effect, the liquidation of the toys and their subsequent free distribution would not be sufficient to meet the needs of all youngsters during childhood. This problem, however, had a solution. For youngsters in the first stages of childhood, that is, from one to ten years of age, the solution was considered so obvious that SUPERCAP's technicians didn't even bother to include it in the supplementary regulations. After all, even if toys could no longer be industrially manufactured, they could still be produced at home. Any mother, no matter how unimaginative, could make a rag doll or stuffed dog out of scraps found in the sewing basket of any home. And the baby would have something to play with. In addition, after mastering motor co-ordination and using the imagination which every child possesses, a youngster could make a little car out of bottle caps and boxes.

As for children over ten years of age, they were formally dealt with by the supplementary regulations for the purposes of logical consideration. They were to play in the country where, pretending to be farmers, they would learn at an early age to love nature and to understand the secrets of agriculture. Without, of course interfering with their school work and class schedule. They would play only during play time. That is: from 7.00–11.00 am when, armed with seeds and light-weight tools, they would healthfully give themselves up to country play under the watchful and competent eyes of a monitor from ASRA (Agricultural Services Recreational Apprenticeship).

Further, it was noted that when the ex-toy makers, benefiting from the financial incentives, began to manufacture the pill, they would be equally entitled to increased production incentives offered to the laboratories already making the pill. However, if they began to profit by these same incentives, then, naturally, they would have to be subject to the same requirements which flowed from these benefits: required minimum levels for the production of the pill. But, while the new and old manufacturers of the pill were obligated in this manner, they were free to raise production levels on their own—as long as it did not require their workers to work more than the normal eight hours plus the permissible three hours of overtime. Besides, regarding personnel, SUPERCAP sent a letter of recommendation to each of the ex-toy manufacturers: in so far as it was possible, existing personnel should be retained. Having new, trained personnel did not invalidate the possibility of utilizing the services of former workers in the toy industry—at least, in the pill packaging department.

The gradual reduction in maternities until their total eradication, a natural, inevitable measure suggested at the outset by CLAN, was approved by SUPERCAP's general assembly and included in the supplementary regulations. If no more babies were to be born, why have motherhood? The question would be pertinent if it didn't already have an answer. The answer began with gradual reduction, which implied a temporary existence for the state of motherhood. And in fact, in the supplementary regulations, a mother's function was guaranteed for the non-renewable period of six months. This tolerance was a result of the birth licences already issued by DEPREGNACC, the validity of which the government, faithful to the principle of a non-retroactive law, recognized and respected. Nonetheless, two restrictive paragraphs were added to the regulations' section dealing with the matter. The first paragraph recommended the strict observance of that which the technicians, using technical terminology, called 'The chronometric flux of the birth licences'. The validity of the birth licences, or the period for which they were in effect, would only be recognized in so far as the conventional gestation period, for statistical purposes, was in accord with the three month base period for eventually doing away with the mandatory abortion phase— except in cases of premature birth. After all, it would be no biological surprise if one day a baby was born at seven months. In itself, the recommendation might have seemed obvious. But clearly it was not so obvious as to have escaped the pragmatic strictness of SUPERCAP's technicians. The second paragraph established that, regardless of the grace period allotted to them, maternity cases would not be referred to as such after 'The Final Measure' went into effect. Actually, the word motherhood had been removed from circulation—and from the dictionary. And, because of the law, or more precisely because of the second paragraph, the old maternity/motherhood cases would be designated

152

simply as 'hospitalization'. In the hospitals already possessing a wing or section designated for maternity cases, steps were immediately taken to remove the signs from the wings and get rid of them.

And the doctors, the obstetricians? Without a doubt, they would have been professionally liquidated if the government hadn't put them under protective status, thus removing another of the decree's secondary effects, or one other residual problem caused by it. With reasonable salaries, and in some cases excellent salaries, the obstetricians were approved for new, optional areas of work which, besides offering them flexibility of adaptation, also guaranteed them job security—and, with job security, the guarantee of survival.

Many of them went to work for CCRIP (Centre for Contraceptive Research to Improve the Pill) where, after a paid internship, they would become part of a team in charge of the project to produce the 'multi-purpose, universal pill'. This project hoped to create one pill designed to take the place of the many types of pill now in use; a pill which, without unpleasant side effects, and, contrariwise, with the advantages of communal efficiency for all somatic types of consumers, would be destined for common use by all Island women. After all, no Island woman should be exposed to side effects from using one type of pill which, although seemingly indicated for her somatic type and which she took because of daring ignorance, actually could only be taken without risk to health and with perfect clinical-consumer performance, by a somatic type different from her own. In this sense, and until the 'multipurpose universal pill' was a reality, a rigorous clinical control also foreseen by the supplementary regulation was to be maintained over the pill's use so that it could only be sold by prescription. Besides, this measure also gave obstetricians another new area of work: at dispensaries, selling the pill in factories and/or businesses with more than 80 female employees, or in pharmacies where the consumers in order to comply with the law, could now have someone at their disposition, authorized by law, to issue the required individual prescription to buy the pill, after the free consultation mandated by the supplementary regulations. In case of organic intolerance, or any other clinical manifestation affecting one's general state of health, and caused by using the pill, the consumer was to immediately return to the doctor issuing her prescription—since his function was not only to prescribe the pill but to give total aid to the clientele in the sense of monitoring the pill's effects and, by extension, the progress of the consumer's clinical chart. In addition to his governmental base salary, the doctor was also paid by pharmacies, industries and businesses under the contraceptive subsidy clause. The clientele should feel at home— even when avoiding the worst.

It's clear that no medical student would think of specializing in obstetrics, nor would this even be possible since obstetrics, according to the supplementary regulations, would be conveniently eradicated from the area of medical specializations. Once the 'multipurpose, universal pill' was perfected, there would be no work even for the old obstetricians who, by controlling the pill's prescription, provisionally carried out their profession up to a certain point—if the 'multipurpose, universal pill' succeeded—they would have to arrange other work outside of the pharmacies and the dispensary booths in factories and industries: in its scientific and consumer universality, the future pill would be sold independent of consultation and prescription. Thus, in addition to becoming perfectly dispensible at that moment, they would also be ineligible for the government's contraceptive subsidy. Nonetheless, the obstetricians approved for work in the labs and for supervising the manufacture of the pill (because it is necessary to note also that, as far as was possible, the obstetricians were certified), would not have their jobs interrupted. The obvious reason: whatever the case, the manufacturers of the 'multipurpose, universal pill' would require supervision, as did the product of any industry which endeavoured to assure quality control—or at least, which wanted responsible manufacturing. For supervising the manufacture of the 'multipurpose, universal pill', the former obstetricians who had had a successful term with

CCRIP in working for the pill's development would receive priority approval. The others would be ranked accordingly. But don't worry: there would be enough jobs for everyone. With the all-out production of the pill, the more supervisors there would be to be pressed promptly into service. Even those obstetricians who might have lost their jobs due to the elimination of prescriptions could be certified—as long as they demonstrated supervisorial skills during their respective terms of service. All this, however, could only be considered at its proper time: after the advent of the 'multipurpose pill'. Until then, and until CCRIP's research indicated that its advent was imminent, the pharmacy, factory and business obstetrician could tranquilly continue on in their roles, and, at their posts, continuing tranquilly to prescribe. After all, should unemployment occur, they were sure that the government would come through with all possible assistance, training them for other areas of work even if not totally related to medical activities, but for which they were suited as demonstrated during their service. Obviously, veterinary service was out of the question for other work areas—at least in so far as this activity was related to obstetrics: no animal needed an obstetrician to give birth. Any animal knew how to do that alone. Besides, if it had enough instinct to do that, no other animal would have enough to help it, if that were the case. The pretence of a human helping a cow or a horse during delivery should be considered as an interruption by men in the animal's natural life. Actually this was done under the pretext of it being a question of thoroughbred stock. But there were no thoroughbreds on the Island. That was prohibited by the government. Now on the Island, instead of thoroughbred animals raised in luxurious barns and stables, there were only poor mortal animals in obscure pastures. Animals fit only for the slaughterhouse. In view of the pre-eminent necessity of provisioning the population, the government, much less the people, could not be interested in breeding thoroughbreds—only in supplies. Even horses were not exempt since people had begun to eat horsemeat, alternating weeks with the beef they had always consumed. There was an end to horse racing which had led to betting and gambling, something which the government, zealous of the popular economy, absolutely would not tolerate. Finally, in addition to eventually becoming beasts of burden, horses had become much more useful to the community, trading jockeys for riders.

(As for dogs, which didn't produce any conveniently consumable meat anyway, they were confined to the ranches where they were specifically used as supportive elements to the hunt and, naturally, to frighten off any intruders with their barking. It must be noted, however, that this canine concession did not apply to show dogs who had been exterminated at the first signs of a food crisis after being formally considered to be parasitic consumers of the already dwindling domestic pantry provisions.)

If the veterinary service, as SPAIT (Services for Professional Adaptation with Intensive Training) had already formally decided, was not the type of activity to which obstetricians could professionally adapt due to the lack of useful services within their professional sphere applicable to animals—this was not the case with paediatrics.

According to SPAIT, while veterinarians and obstetricians incidentally implied a monopoly, shaped by the specific physical act of reproduction, which led the animal to give birth without any assistance other than that of its generic instinct, and women to give birth with the obstetrician's professional help or the assistance of the midwife, each one, woman and animal, bearing children in their manner, but ultimately giving birth—paediatrics and veterinary services implied not an isolated situation in common, but a whole line of situational occurrences, defined in terms of inclusive analogous situations, sensitively compatible in so far as they were common to the child and to animal young: the nursing of young, their innocent mischiefs, the cares which the two inspired during their apprenticeship of day-to-day living on similar planes of vigilant devotion, leading the bitch to protect her pups and the woman to care for her child, which, by analogy, was her pup.

Obviously, after children ceased to exist—their natural, small clientele—and after an easy period of adjustment, the paediatricians could easily perform related services in the veterinary field, accompanying the growth of young animals so that they would be strong and healthy and grow to be conveniently fat and robust.

Nonetheless, because of the supplementary regulations, and following the obstetrician's example, paediatrics also suffered a curricular veto in the field of medical teaching. However, paediatricians were conceded a longer deadline of six years from the start of the decree's effect in order that they might freely practice and attend any children who might be born during the post-decree period, including in this service, naturally, those who were infants when 'The Final Measure' was handed down. Afterwards, it was a transfer to the veterinary field, although they still had the option of transferring there before the deadline expired.

Returning to the subject of fiscal incentives offered for increased production of the pill, one must note that SUPERCAP did not make them a part of the supplementary regulations as strict industrial data, objectifying simply the relationship between the pill's production and the demand index on the level of an increase in consumer necessities brought about by the mandatory use of the pill. Actually, SUPERCAP considered the incentives in terms of a total strategy of benefits which did not exclude favouring the popular economy. Increasing the pill's production levels was not destined solely to adjust supply and demand levels with the specific objective of providing pills to the consumers, who were obliged by law to take them anyway; it would have been unjust, therefore, for the government not to have laid in an ample supply so that women could regularly obtain the pill, and in doing so, comply with the law to the fullest. This was the least that they could do. The government, however, in increasing the pill's production so that no consumer would go without, also created conditions in which the pill, because of increased production resulting in lower industrial costs—was placed on the market at a lower uniform price. It was exactly for this reason that the theory of graduated economics was formulated and TECOPRICO (Technical Commission for Price Controls) was created.

Because of the incentives, one more problem was thus resolved: the problem of the pill's cost in relation to the popular economy. Nonetheless, it would be redesigned with the advent of the future 'multipurpose, universal pill' which, purporting to avoid the industrial proliferation of the pill caused by the manufacture of diverse brands, would concentrate all the industry's production on one type of pill destined for generalized contraceptive use, freeing consumers from the consultation and prescription routine. Not to mention the benefits to the graduated economy resulting from the product's commercial price as a direct consequence of lower industrial costs caused by the non-diversified increase in production, now efficiently concentrating on a single product—the universal, singular pill. Actually, no matter how much more costly the industrial expenses of the future pill, and they were bound to be more, they wouldn't raise the price by more than 7.5 per cent or 8.3 per cent of the fixed price of the pill in use, as established by TECOPRICO's price controls. There was no doubt: without the benefits of a graduated economy, the fixed price of the pill—the 'multipurpose, universal pill'—would be much higher, perhaps 30 to 40 per cent higher. These were the conclusions reached by CARRIF (Council for the Application of Resources with Retroactive Investment of Funds) in their findings of the investigative prospectus. In short, all this proved that the government was preoccupied by providing the incentive strategy with not only a dimension of total inclusiveness, but with a fabric of versatile universality embracing everything from scientific research to retail outlets.

Only one point was lacking from the incentives: the male contraceptive pill. Initial research at first undertaken by a small but persistent group of scientists in their free time was suspended by government order before the findings were officially forwarded to the Council Director of that noble, hard-working centre of studies. Once 'The Final Measure' was in effect, the suspension order was modified by a CVP (Confidential Veto Power) which prohibited any and all scientists in or outside of CCRIP from pursuing that line of research under penalty of imprisonment and suspension of licence. Because it was a question of a confidential ordinance, its classified content was secretly eliminated from the text of the supplementary regulations. There was no reason it shouldn't have been unless the CVP wasn't a CVP but a simple VP (Veto Power). Anyway, SUPERCAP, which never adopted a measure without first explaining why, made explicit the reasons for the aforementioned CVP in a special memo. The reasons were quite convincing: if the woman conceived the child and the problem was stopping conception, it would be unfair for the man to have to submit to taking the pill, under the pretext of the woman avoiding conception of a child which could not be conceived by a man, but only by her. Besides, supposing the male contraceptive pill were developed and put to use, what would be the woman's status in the community? One must not forget that the woman, by her taking the pill instead of the man, assumed a noble attitude *vis-à-vis* the community which no one could deny her and of which she—unless she were a moron—should be deeply conscious and proud: the nobility of renouncing fertility, to save the community from hunger caused by the population explosion. And, naturally, renouncing fertility made her that much more noble since the man was still able to fertilize her. This argument, while considered valid, was not the factor which prevailed over the formally legal reason invoked by SUPERCAP to condemn research into the male contraceptive pill: if the law mandated that conception be prevented by the use of the pill, let it be taken not by the man who could not conceive, but by the woman who did bear the children.

This did not mean that a woman, eventually giving up the pill put preserving the contraceptive mandate—couldn't have her tubes tied if she wanted. Besides giving women this option, if the husband consented, in the supplementary regulation the government guaranteed her a 15 per cent discount on that expensive operation.

But with such complex measures for its execution, with the decree's complicated regulatory dynamics which permitted the incentive of a 15 per cent discount on the hospital bill and the eventual tying off of a woman's tubes, wouldn't it be easier for the government to mandate mass sterilization for women?

Sterilization?

Who said anything about sterilization?

Can we have heard right?

Let's not mention sterilization.

No one can—nor could—talk about sterilization.

It was prohibited to mention sterilization on the Island.

The technocracy rejected simplistic solutions.

And the Island lived under a technocracy.

Mass sterilization?

That's all they needed!

And the organization?

And organizationality?

And the structures?

And the infra-structures?

And the information systems?

And the subsystems?

And the alternatives?

And the variables?

And the unknowns?

And the retroactive investments?

And the graduated economy?

And the parameters?

And the visual recodifying?

No! The Island was a technocracy. And being a technocracy, all the problems were to be resolved, not simplistically, at the level of a layman's simplistic view, but at a technical level, by technicians. A complex problem such as the population explosion demanded a correspondingly complex solution. A wide-spread problem, such as controlling the birthrate, in turn required a comprehensive solution. And, as it was a question of interrelated problems, the technicians could only resolve them in the manner in which they had done: by complicated, comprehensive measures, in so far as they were comprehensively complex.

Five days elapsed between the announcement of the decree with its basic regulations and the publication of the supplementary regulations. Everything which happened during those days, or which was related to those events, has been related. It didn't rain on any of those day. They were beautiful days. Blue skies, sunny days. Under the sun, the Island entered a new era: something new had begun under the sun.

PART III

The Book of the Son

'There is nothing new under the sun.'
ECCLESIASTES

Teodorico and his Companions

1. And Teodorico met with his companions who, like him, had humble professions, and worked in their homes; which were also their workshops. Actually, they lived in the workshops, each one caring for his craft.

2. Almost all the people worked in great factories; which had employment for almost all people. Then, modern machines, perfect in all things, were installed in the great factories: they were machines that could alone produce what it took many people working together to produce.

3. Then, many people were fired from the great factories; among them, Teodorico and his companions.

4. The great factories' production rose greatly; the number of unemployed rose greatly, also. In truth, the people dismissed from the great factories had no jobs.

5. Then the government passed a law; which was considered saving. According to the new law, the factories reduced the production of their modern machines, perfect in all things.

6. By this means, the government created jobs for many people; because the people dismissed from the great factories returned to work as they had before: each one caring for his craft, outside of the great factories. Because it was this way before, and was to be afterwards: work which the hand makes, by the hand must be made.

7. Then, production was divided; and this was the division: the great factories were charged with the major part of production; and the minor part of production was left to the people who no longer worked in the great factories.

8. The important thing was that production did not exceed the people's need for those products. In truth, this is what happened; and, having happened, what was produced was utilized.

9. The great factories had their production under control; and those who did not work there worked on a contract basis; which meant that they produced only what they were contracted to produce.

10. The contract complemented the stockpiling of things which the people needed; they were met by the great factories' production, and by the work of those who had been fired.

Humble Professions

11. And there was work for all, even for those who had humble professions. In truth, no

office is so humble that it does not have its importance.

12. And the importance of the humble professions lay in the utilization of people to fix the great factories' products; which, having been made by them, were not repaired by them. Actually, the great factories only manufactured products; and, if the great factories only made them, they could not waste time fixing them. Because they were made to be worn out.

13. Thus Teodorico, after being dismissed from the shoe factory, returned to resoling worn out shoe soles; and Estêvão the tinker, returned to repairing the pots made by the domestic utensil factory where he had worked; since, they, too, wore out.

14. The same thing happened to the other companions, who also had humble professions: the same thing happened to Pedro, the lathe operator; and to Joseph, the carpenter. Because there was a carpenter named Joseph who, dismissed from the furniture factory, now lived by fixing furniture. And his profession was humble, as was that of his companions.

15. And, having returned to their humble crafts, they also were called by their first names again; because in the great factories, when they still worked there, they had been known by numbers instead of names; and they were called by bells. Actually, only the great factories had names, and not those who worked in them.

The Anniversary

16. And Teodorico met with his companions to celebrate his son's birthday; who, being a boy, had taken the same name as his father, just as he had foreseen, it being his desire and will. And on that day his son was two years old.

17. And Estêvão, the tinker, came with his wife; and Pedro, the lathe operator, also brought his wife; and they brought their children. Because they had come to celebrate the birthday of the son of Teodorico, the cobbler. And everyone was happy about the birthday which brought them all together, they and their children.

18. In fact, only Joseph, the carpenter, came alone; because of the three he was the only one not to have a wife or children.

19. But, Joseph was also happy about the birthday. His heart told him one thing, though: he would be happier if he weren't there alone. Because, even though he was with the others, he was solitary.

20. And it happened that a few days earlier, Teodorico's wife had received a visit from one of her cousins: she came from the country to try and get work in the city.

21. The cousin's name was Mary. And she said: Cousin, I don't have anyone to look after me as I did before. Because my father, your uncle, has died. I didn't have a mother, and now I don't have a father. The dove

166

lost in the storm can't feel any more alone than I do. Because my parents didn't have any other children besides myself; they didn't give me any brothers or sisters. The winds of the storm brought me here.

22. The two embraced and cried. Teodorico's wife, Isabel, said to Mary: My home is yours: not only for today, tomorrow, and the next day; but for as long as is necessary, until you get a job. But don't let even that stop you from staying here.

23. Isabel's offer was sincere; she had a warm heart, full of goodness.

24. Then, Mary answered: Since it's all right with you, I'll stay here. I don't know how to thank you. I'll say only one thing: I hope I live many years so that I may have time to demonstrate my gratitude during them. Because, no matter the days, weeks or years that may pass, I can never forget your generosity in letting me stay with you in your home.

25. And Isabel said to her: The little I've done for you is not to be mentioned. Because, in opening the door to my house to you, I have only opened the door to your own home. Never forget that.

26. And Mary came to live in her cousin's house; and she helped with the preparations for the party; the cookies, the candy, the cake. The guests praised the table decorations: simple, but artfully arranged with good taste. On top of the cake was a little almond paste doll, resting on yellow icing that looked like straw. And he was so well made, with his little arms wide open as though extended in a plea for tenderness, that everyone was curious to know who made it. And Isabel said: It was Cousin Mary.

27. Then she introduced her cousin to the guests. And thus it was that Joseph, the carpenter, came to be acquainted with Mary.

The Predestined Ones

28. And Joseph looked at Mary who was pleasing to his eyes and to his heart. And Joseph was pleasing to Mary's eyes and heart. And being the only ones who were there alone, they didn't feel as solitary as before. Because when they saw each other, something spoke to their hearts: each was the part missing in the other, needed to complement one another and form a whole, one existence of dedication and love.

29. A mutual feeling of love blossomed in their hearts, as sudden as it was profound. And when this happens, there is no more solitude. Because no solitude is worse than that of the solitary heart.

30. Truly, it was as though they had found each other after searching for a long time: Mary and Joseph, no longer acquaintances, but predestined from long ago: in the wind, in the stars of the sky, in the flowers of the fields, in the mountain streams —in each other's hearts.

The Meeting under the Chestnut Tree

31. And it happened that two days later, Joseph met Mary, who by accident, was crossing the park. They walked together and sat down under a chestnut tree.

32. And Joseph said to her: I've dreamed about you for two nights. You are always in my heart, and in my dreams: even when I sleep, I think about you.

33. And Mary said to him: I've also thought about you all this time. And, even now, seeing you here, it's as if I was dreaming. Really, it's like a dream to have us both here, beside each other, sitting on this park bench. I didn't expect to see you before Sunday; on Sundays, my cousin tells me that you usually come to Teodorico's house.

34. And Joseph said to her: That's right. But if that were the only way to see you, my weeks would be too long. My eyes can't go so long without seeing you. It's not enough that in your absence I see you in my heart. Because it's with the eyes that see the moon in the sky, and the acacias blooming in the woods, and the willows at the edge of the lake—I also want to see you with those eyes.

35. And Mary said to him: Well, if that is so, enjoy it now, because I'm here with you; rest the eyes, which see so many beautiful things, on me, and I hope that they will not be disenchanted with what they see.

36. And Joseph said to her: My eyes have not seen, nor will they see, anything as beautiful as you are to me now. Nothing that they have seen equals the beauty of your face: not the moon in the sky, nor the acacias in bloom, nor the willows of the lake. But they will not be satisfied with seeing you only today. They want to see you every day of the year: all year, all my life. And when they close for the last time, they will still not have grown tired of seeing you.

37. And Mary asked him: How can your eyes look at me for the rest of your life if I'm not sure that I will continue to live in the city?

38. And Joseph answered her: You won't leave here without me. And if I stay here, you will, too. Because we already know one thing, in our hearts: you are me, and I am you. And nothing can divide what is inseparable.

39. And seeing that Mary was silent, Joseph continued: Your silence frightens me. Is it that you don't want me as your husband? You have free will: only you can now decide what your father would have had to decide if he were alive. I'm asking for your hand, Mary.

40. And Mary said to him: Your words fall on my heart as the rain on the fields. And as the fields are reborn in silence after the rain, my heart has been reborn again in silence after hearing your words. And how can I answer you if not with my silence? But now I will answer:

you asked for my hand, and I give it to you freely.

41. And, in a gesture of moving tenderness, Mary extended her hand, and Joseph took it lovingly between his own. And they agreed that on Sunday they would announce their betrothal in Teodorico's house.

The Lovers

42. And that is what they did. And everyone was happy about their engagement. And they had known each other and fallen in love in such a short time that to the others it didn't seem hasty, but good and beautiful. Because the sun doesn't need much time to rise. And when something has to happen, it happens, no matter if the time involved is short or long. And it can only appear hasty to one who doubts that it is happening in its proper time. But no one thought about Mary and Joseph's engagement.

43. And no one thought that about the marriage; it was set for two months later since this was the time considered necessary to complete the arrangements and comply with legal formalities. And the lovers didn't wait any longer than was necessary for the marriage.

44. And Joseph filled out the authorities' form requesting permission to marry. Because without written permission from the authorities, no one could get married. And on the permit, the groom had to declare and prove his monthly salary, and wait for the authorities' investigation.

Because only those who earned enough money could get a marriage licence from the authorities.

45. And if it happened that he didn't earn enough each month, he could add his monthly salary to that of his bride if she had saved up some money from working. The authorities granted the groom this right. And in this case, the bride was required to submit her own permit, even if the authorities did consider it jointly with that of the groom.

46. And since Mary was still unemployed, she was exempted from the requirement. Actually, Joseph did earn enough to get the marriage licence from the authorities. However, more than a month passed before the authorities concluded their investigation; being favourable, it granted them the licence.

47. And stapled to the licence was a sheet entitled 'The Final Measure'; it was the decree of the same name, prohibiting women to have children.

The Wedding

48. And during that month and the following, Joseph was putting the house in order to receive Mary. And, armed with the licence, he appeared with his bride before the magistrate who married them in the presence of witnesses. The witnesses were: Teodorico, the cobbler; Estêvão, the tinker; and Pedro, the lathe operator. And their wives were also present, who,

169

along with the newly-wed Mary, formed four couples. And the men and the women rejoiced in this.

49. After leaving the magistrate, they all went to Joseph's house to celebrate the wedding; and the house was now Mary's, too; because, belonging to one another, by heart and by marriage, what belonged to one belonged to the other, equally shared, in their shared life. Because for a life together, with shared joy and sorrow, they had been predestined.

50. And to celebrate the wedding, there was lamb, wine and bread. And Joseph gave food and drink to all. And everyone ate and drank, and toasted one another. And they did so as a sign of rejoicing.

51. And, after the guests had gone, Mary and Joseph were alone. But they weren't solitary: because they weren't solitary from the moment in which they saw each other. And no man or woman is alone when love is with them. And love was with Mary and Joseph and being with them, it was in them: in their gestures, in their looks, in their words, in their hearts. As the light of the lamp, and the perfume of the rose. And, as two, they became one.

The Revelation

1. And it happened that one afternoon, when he came home, Joseph found Mary crying. And he asked her why she cried. And she answered: I'm crying for joy and for fear.'

2. And he said to her: If you are happy enough to be crying for joy, how could you also be crying out of fear?

3. And Mary answered him: What is making me cry is the fear of my joy. Because what today makes my heart rejoice, tomorrow can be the cause of my sorrow. This is what I fear.

4. And, having dried her eyes with her hand, Mary slowly raised them to Joseph, and fixed them on his. And then the light Joseph saw in Mary's eyes did not come from hers, nor from her heart, but from the depths of her being. It wasn't the same light that he was accustomed to seeing in her eyes. This is how it seemed to him for a moment.

5. And Joseph had a premonition. And he asked her: How can you be pregnant? And he said to her: It makes me happy, too, but it also makes me afraid, like you. You know the law. You must go to the medical authorities before it is too late.

6. And on that very afternoon, at the last hour, Joseph took Mary to the medical authorities. And they examined her. And they said to her: You are pregnant. And this proves that you haven't been taking the pill, as the law requires. You have broken the law.

7. Then Mary protested, saying that she had never broken the law. And the medical authorities said to her: We will see. It doesn't do any good to assure us that you regularly took the pill. We have ways of proving if you are telling the truth or lying. The

examination will prove it.

8. And they sent a sample of Mary's blood to be tested. And in the sample they found the substance of which the pill was made. Because at that time only one type of pill was in use which, serving its own ends, indifferently served all women. Thus, it was impossible for a woman who used the pill to become pregnant.

9. And when they saw the results of the examination, the medical authorities said to Mary: This is singularly strange. The examination proves that you really have been using the pill regularly. And having done so, how could you have become pregnant? This is the first time that this has happened. Whatever the reason, you will have to get an abortion. We'll do it tomorrow. Be here at nine o'clock.

10. And with these words, they dismissed Mary, who returned home with Joseph.

Mary and Joseph's Decision

11. And it was evening when they arrived home. And Mary told Joseph all about the conversation she had had with the medical authorities. And she told him about the time of the appointment for the abortion. And she said to him: It's the law, you know. But my heart tells me that I will have to break the law. Because this is my destiny, and it must be served.

12. And Joseph said to her: You have the law's decision. But I will tell you one thing: the decision you make will be mine.

13. And his words were sincere, and there was no fear in them. Because when he said them, fear disappeared from his heart. And his words came from his heart.

14. And he said: What has been conceived in you, should not be, but since it is, I take it as a sign. Because it is a sign that love can triumph over inequity.

15. And Mary said to him: You are a just man. And from me will be born the child which you fathered. If nothing stopped you from fathering it, nothing will stop me from having it. Because destiny must be fulfilled, and he will be born as testimony to that fact.

16. And having decided that, they did what seemed to be right and true. Because they knew that nothing else was to be done; and that it is right and true to do something that you believe in.

17. And it happened that on the next day Mary did not appear at the medical authorities: not at the appointment time, nor afterward. And the medical authorities thought that it was suspicious that she did not appear. Because the day and the time had been set for her abortion, as the law mandated.

18. Then the medical authorities communicated this fact to the Chief of Police. And an officer went to Mary's house to force her to go. And he found the house locked.

19. And the house remained isolated, although there were other houses in the vicinity. And

when the officer interrogated the people living there, he found out that Mary and Joseph's house had been locked from sunrise of that day: some people had noticed it, and had reported it early.

20. And the officer returned with the information, and transmitted it to the Chief; he said: They must have gone out for some reason, and for some reason, their return has been delayed. Since it's late, I'll send someone over to see them tomorrow. And they will have to explain why they were gone for so long.

21. And it happened that the officer, returning the next day, found the house still locked as before. And he knocked at the door, and no one opened. And he noticed that there was no sign of life in the house. And having so noted, he so testified to the Chief.

22. Then, the Chief sent three officers to the neighbourhood, and gave them orders to break into the house; once entered, there was no one inside. And the few things left indicated that its inhabitants had abandoned it.

23. And, finding out about this, the Chief sent for the couple's friends; because to know everything about someone, you had to know their friends. And the best way to find out the couple's hiding place was to ask their friends.

24. And he summoned Teodorico to his office, and Estêvão, and Pedro; and their wives, too. And he interrogated each of them, one by one.

25. And each was surprised; because they didn't know anything about what had happened. And in their statements, there were no contradictions; because, intimidated into telling the truth, they told only the truth. And the truth was one: none of them knew that Mary and Joseph had abandoned the house, nor did they know where they were hiding.

26. Then the Police Chief dismissed them, although he put them under surveillance. And from that day forward, all their actions were watched. Because not knowing something in a day does not mean that you will not learn something later on. And a simple act can anticipate a word, which could lead to the truth. And what words hide, an act can reveal.

27. That is why their actions were watched.

Other Measures

28. On the same day, the Police Chief sent warnings to other locations; and in all the places there were authorities; which, receiving the notice, tried to put into effect his orders.

29. And the order was to watch the comings and goings of the people, and examine their documents; because a woman named Mary, who had broken the law, had disappeared; and it was necessary to find her. And her husband, named Joseph, accompanied her, and he was a carpenter. Everything indicated

172

that the two had fled, and were in collusion against the law.

30. And the authorities did it, in all locales. And they put every effort into their surveillance.

31. But the Chief of Police also took other measures which seemed more efficient. The measure consisted of the following: he chose his two best officers, who were tracers; he immediately sent them out with orders to sniff out all the Island's hiding places: the brush, the hills, the swamps; because the fugitives, fearful of being caught, were sure to be well-hidden. And only in one of these places would it be possible. And these two officers knew these places better than anyone else.

32. And to fulfill their mission the two officers left, taking two bloodhounds with them; which, having proved themselves in many hunts, were the best of the canine corps.

The Flight

1. And it happened that Joseph and Mary had really fled, because they had had to; and they did so on the morning of the first day, when everyone was still asleep. From the little they possessed they took only the necessities. And Joseph carried his work tools.

2. And they locked the house that they had lived in.

3. And they avoided the roads, taking unmapped paths where only the animals passed. Because they didn't want to be seen by anyone.

4. And for many, many days, they lost themselves in the brush, and slept out of doors. Joseph had a plan in mind, and he told it to Mary. But to carry it out, they first had to reach the sea.

5. And not knowing which direction to take to get there, they followed the mountains; because from on top of one of them, they should be able to see the sea. And the mountains were far away.

6. And it happened that the mountains were farther away than they had imagined. For many, many days they walked, and did not reach them, although they continued to see them, hazy in the distance.

7. But each day they felt their strength ebbing. And they couldn't walk as far, and broke up the day with longer and longer rest intervals. And this delayed their arrival at the mountains.

8. And it happened that one day Mary fell down, exhausted. Her feet were swollen and painful, her lips cracked with thirst. And she asked Joseph to moisten them with the rest of the water in the flask.

9. But the flask was empty. Then, Joseph went out to look for water; and he found it in a pool, where he filled the flask. And he gave water to Mary, and he said to her: We will stay here until you get your strength back. You are suffering from malnutrition because, since our supplies ran out, I have only been able to give you wild fruits

173

and roots.

10. And Mary answered him: You have done what you have always done: share your food with me. And you have had nothing else, either.

11. Then Joseph carried her over to a bamboo grove, near where she had fallen. And there in the shade of the bamboo, he left her.

12. Then he cut down a pole; and, with a line and a hook that he had brought in his pack, he hurried back to the pool; which was the first one they had found for many days. And, having used the pool to bring water to Mary, he hoped to find fish in it also, and bring them to her to feed her. And he said this to himself as he walked back to the pool.

13. And, arriving at the edge of the pool, he dug down into the earth in search of worms; and, having found some, he prepared the bait. He threw the hook into the pool. And, thinking about his wife's hunger, and about the hunger of the child she carried in her belly, he felt his heart swell with pity for the two. And his pity was so great, that his heart ached.

14. While this was going on, Mary waited in the bamboo grove. And in vain she tried to calculate the number of days that had passed since they ran away. And, having lost track of the days, she calculated the time by the increasing size of her belly, poking it and staring at it. And it seemed to her that three months had passed already.

15. And, although she was hungry, and still far from the mountains, she didn't worry. And she said to herself: The law's injustice will not prevail over me. And let not my enemies rejoice in my difficult circumstances. Because what is difficult today, will not be so tomorrow.

16. And it happened that Joseph caught a large fish. And, making a fire, he roasted it on a stick. And he ate it with Mary.

17. And for three days they rested in the bamboo grove, eating fish. Because the pool was full of fish; and they did not lack for fish during those three days.

18. But after they started their journey again, the pool dried up. And, because Joseph did not return to the pool, he never knew what had happened.

19. And they didn't know about the other extraordinary things which happened afterwards. Because what happened was not for them to know.

20. And one of those things was this: as Joseph and Mary walked on, birds flew down to the ground to hunt for food; and as they foraged, they covered up the tracks that the two had left.

21. And one of the other things was this: one day they came to a pool, crossing it without apparent danger; actually, it was inhabited by alligators who had hidden themselves in the vegetation and let them pass.

22. And thus, without knowing, they fled in safety. Because they were sure of themselves. And, being preoccupied with

thoughts of the child that was to be born, they didn't think about anything bad that could happen to them. Because, in thinking only about the child, they thought only about the good.

23. And it happened that one day, after having come through dense thickets, they came to a clearing where there was an old house standing in ruins. Mary trembled with emotion and surprise. And she said to Joseph: I know this place. The village where I was born is not far from here. How strange that my steps have brought me back to my land. But I cannot return home.

24. And Joseph said to her: We will take another route.

25. And, as they were without food, Mary answered him: Let us wait until I try and get some food from that house; not for me, but for our child. But first, let me make sure that the same man still lives there that I knew in my childhood. Let's hide behind those bushes. Maybe I can see him.

26. And they did so.

27. And, as they watched the house, Mary said to Joseph: According to what my grandfather told me, that house was once a church. But I knew it when it was a pottery barn. I was here one or two times with my grandfather. Actually, then it wasn't so run down; now, I see that it's barely standing. The man who used to live here—and I also found this out through my grandfather—used to be a priest, who became a potter.

28. And, hardly had Mary finished speaking, when an old man appeared at the door; who was dressed like any other person, making it difficult to believe that he had ever been a priest; since, as one knows, when there were priests, they dressed differently than other people, and were identifiable as priests.

29. And, Mary and Joseph knew that there were no priests left, nor anyone who had been one. Because, since several decades had passed since religion had been eliminated, all the priests had died. And he, without a doubt, was the last; and he was so by virtue of having reached an age which no one else had reached.

30. And perhaps he had reached that age because he was not to die until he had done a good deed. And perhaps he could do that now. Because perhaps for this reason, fate had spared him, and given him a long life.

31. And, thinking this, Mary said so to Joseph. And the two walked toward the house.

32. Then, seeing Mary's condition, the old priest said to her: I see that you are the sinner that I heard about in the village this morning, when I was there making some purchases for my poor pantry. Because it is difficult to believe that more than one woman would have dared to break the law. But you have come to my poor home, and I ask you: what can you want from a poor old man like myself?

175

33. And Mary answered him: I desire nothing more than your compassion. Take pity on me and my husband. Do not say that you've seen us. Because our lives will be in danger if they find out that we were here. And if you can offer us a little bit of food, I will not refuse it.

34. And the old priest said to her: You can have the food I will give you.

35. And, giving them some potatoes and a hunk of meat, he asked Mary: Why did you look for me so confidently?

36. And Mary answered: Because when I was a little girl, I met you on this very spot. And I knew that you had been one of God's servants.

37. And for the first time she remembered the word 'God'. Because, when she had seen the old priest, she remembered it. Actually, neither her generation nor that of her father had known it. She had only known about it when her grandfather mentioned it on the day he had spoken about the old priest.

38. And the old man said to her: Yes, I really was a servant of God. But the time of the kingdom of God has passed. In place of God's kingdom, we have the administration of men. And I cannot stop being a man of my time just because I am old. Because my time is the time in which I live.

39. And so saying, he made a motion as if to close the door. But, he said to Mary: Don't prolong our conversation unnecessarily. I gave you the food

you asked for. I now ask you for something: go right away. Don't let your presence get an old man like myself in trouble.

40. And he closed the door in their faces.

41. And they followed a path and disappeared. And for two days they walked toward the mountains which were now close.

42. And it happened that when they finally reached the foothills, they saw a small donkey pastured there. And Joseph approached the donkey which did not flee.

43. And then Joseph, seeing his gentleness, tied one of the cords he had brought around the donkey's neck. And he put Mary, who was tired, on the donkey's back.

44. And pulling the donkey by the cord, he began to climb the mountains step by step. And Mary rested against the pack and saddlebags that Joseph had tied to the donkey's back.

45. And it happened that, arriving finally at the top of the mountains, they saw the sea below. Then they began the descent, always aided by the gentle donkey.

46. And they took refuge in a cave they had found by chance, just a few steps from the sea.

47. And there they stayed for many, many days, which turned into weeks. And Joseph improvised a little work area in the cave where he dragged wood cut down from some trees in a nearby forest.

48. And, with the tools that

he had brought, he worked to build a boat. At night, when the schools of fish came to the rocks, he would fish. And they lived on fish and wild fruits—he and Mary.

49. And she, almost ready to give birth, would go out every morning to fill the flask at a nearby spring which they had found during the first exploration around the cave.

50. And it happened that one afternoon, when there was a storm, a cow wandered into the cave seeking shelter. And Mary and Joseph, who had been outside and were returning to the cave during the storm, found her there. And taking pity on her, they sheltered her. Because, like the donkey, she was a gentle animal.

51. And the two small and docile animals must have been lost from some herd. And, because they were lost, they were found by Mary and Joseph. And, although they were found on different occasions and under different circumstances, they received the same treatment from Mary and Joseph.

52. And they were so well-treated, that they developed an affection for them; and there they stayed to keep them company. And at night, they kept them warm with their breath which was warm and strong.

53. And during those days and weeks, no one saw the cave's inhabitants. Because no one went to that place. And they lived in peace and were safe.

The Ruined House

1. And it happened that some days after Mary and Joseph left the old priest, two officers came to him. And the two officers had already searched many places, seeking the fugitives. And, although they were tracers, they had not found any sign of them anywhere.

2. And the two officers interrogated the old priest: they wanted to know if the sinner had passed that way. Because, since she had been born in the neighbouring village and had lived for many years in one nearby, she must know the region well. And knowing it well, she must be hidden there.

3. And the old priest answered them: You are men of the law. And man cannot live without laws; and that's why they are made. Let the law be carried out, then.

4. And, finishing his answer, he told them that the fugitives had passed by there. He could not deny it. And he asked them to leave him alone because he was a poor old man. And, taking his leave, he pointed to the mountains, and said to them: There. They must have gone to the mountains. They couldn't have chosen any other place to hide because down here, on the plains, they would easily be found.

5. Then the officers, after having given him three pieces of silver, left with their dogs on their way to the mountains.

6. But they had hardly gone

more than a few feet when behind them they heard a great noise, and they turned around. And they were afraid of what they saw: the old priest's house, which had been partially destroyed before, had totally caved in, buring him under the débris. In its place, there was now a pile of bricks and broken boards standing in the midst of a great cloud of dust, utterly silent.

7. And one of the officers said to the other: It's lucky that before he died, he had time to do one good deed by telling us what he knew about the sinner.

8. And the two resumed their trek.

The Discovery

1. And, finally arriving at the foothills, the officers first began to explore in various directions, searching in vain for the fugitive's tracks. Then, they began to climb the mountains. And they began a search that was as minute as it was slow. Because, not finding any trace of the fugitive's passing, they thought it wise to search every cave that they found on the way up.

2. And, as they had to spend part of their time hunting animals for food, the search became even more prolonged.

3. And it happened that, having reached the summit of the mountains in their fruitless search of the caves, they began the descent to the sea. And they searched every path they found, and entered every cave they saw. And they did so because it seemed wise to do on the descent what they had done during the ascent. Because they were convinced of one thing: if the sinner was hiding in the hills, they would find her.

4. And it happened that one day they found a cave near the sea, and they set the dogs on it; who, baying furiously, ran to the cave's entrance. But when they entered, they stopped barking.

5. And, when the officers reached the cave's entrance, they stopped suddenly, perplexed. Because they saw something that they could not have imagined: lying on some straw, arms waving, smiling, was a baby; and on one side stood a cow, and on the other, a donkey; and bent over the child were a man and a woman, looking at it with such tenderness, that they didn't see the men enter.

6. And at the feet of the baby lay the two dogs, with their heads silently resting on their paws.

7. Then, totally confused, the officer who had commented on the priest's end, asked the woman: What is your name?

8. And she answered him: Mary.

9. And the officer said to her: You made us waste a lot of time looking for you. But, all is not lost, because we have found you. You are accused of breaking the law. I have brought the paper you will have to sign before the execution. Because my orders are to kill you and your child.

10. And Mary said to him: You may kill me, but not my

child, who is only one month old, and innocent.

11. And the officer said to her: Your child has only made your crime worse. Because if it was wrong to have borne him, it would be worse to let him live. And that is why he will die first.

12. And, no sooner had he spoken these words, than the officer unsheathed his sword and walked toward the child.

13. Then Joseph cried: No! You cannot do such a thing. Kill me, and let my wife and child live.

14. And it happened then that the other officer, having felt sorry for the child, said to his companion: Do not do it!

15. And the other answered him: I do not understand you. Are you on their side, or the law's?

16. And, so saying, he raised his arm to strike the child with his sword.

17. But, at the same time, he fell, mortally wounded. Because his companion, to save the child, had shot him in the heart.

18. Then Mary threw herself at the child and took him in her arms. And she began to cry.

19. And the officer said to her: I must finish what I have begun. If I saved your child, I must also save you and your husband. Because this child needs two parents to live. And I will not be the one to take them from him.

20. And suddenly seeing the boat in the cave, he asked Joseph: What do you plan to do with that boat?

21. And Joseph answered him: I just finished building it two weeks ago. I was waiting for the baby to be one month old before we fled over the sea. Since the beginning, this has been my plan.

22. And the officer said to him: How could you have believed in such a foolish plan? Since the time of the great earthquakes which destroyed the world, there has only been the Island. There is nothing else across the sea. And if you escape by crossing the sea, you condemn your wife and son to death, because you will not find any place to land.

23. And Joseph answered him: It will not matter if we die together on the sea, because we will be dying far from here. And that is what matters. Because there has been a superior force which has been pushing us towards the unknown from the beginning. And it is to the unknown that we will testify of the injustice which reigns over this Island.

24. And the officer said to him: I do not understand. I see, however, that you know what you are talking about. And my not understanding you is no more important than you understanding yourself. Go. But leave as soon as possible, because others may be on your track and no one will stop you. Because no one can stop me, either, from doing what I must.

25. Then Joseph, with the officer's help, put the boat up on log rollers; and he tied the

donkey and the cow to the boat to pull it. And he and the officer went along repositioning the rollers so that the boat would slide along them. And doing so, they got the boat to the sea.

26. And Joseph, who had put his things in the boat along with the provisions that the officer gave him, put in the oars and had Mary and the child come aboard, and then he set sail. It was dusk already. Then Joseph said to Mary: I will row all night. By daybreak, we will be far from here.

27. And the boat was already pulling away when they heard a shot. And they turned around. Then they saw the guard, who had been killed, fall from high on a rock into the sea.

What came from the Sea

1. And it happened that 30 years later, when a ragged multitude was meeting on the beach one morning, that they saw a light come from the sea.

2. And the light which approached then took on human form. But it did not cease to shine; because there was something like a halo of intense luminosity crowning the man into which the light had formed.

3. And the man had on a white tunic, and had a long beard and long hair.

4. And everyone saw him and looked at him; and they retreated, afraid: because the man was walking on the sea as though he were on land.

5. And as he approached the beach, the multitude retreated further and further. And many were the first to run to the square to tell the authorities about what they had seen.

6. Then, when he reached the sand, no one was left. Because everyone had run to the square. And they had done so in search of safety. Because in the square were the buildings where the high authorities resided; which were securely protected by the guards.

7. And it happened that the man from the sea went there, too. And the high authorities, leaving their work, ran to the windows to see him. And they saw him walking without his feet touching the ground; and over his head they saw the halo of light.

8. Then, he stopped in the middle of the square, and was surrounded by the multitude who shivered in fear; and opening his arms, he asked: Where are the children?

9. And his voice was heard by all, because it echoed over the Island like a thunder clap from heaven.

10. And again his voice echoed as he said: Come unto me little children.

11. And it happened that, at the same instant, all the Island trembled. And the buildings of the square where the high authorities resided collapsed. And the chimneys of the great factories caved in, and all their installations.

12. And from the débris, as though hatching out of egg

shells, began to come the children.

13. And in flocks they approached him; because they were not afraid like the people were. And they had come to answer his call.

14. Then the multitude fled in terror to the mountains. And not only those who had been in the square. Because those who had been in other parts of the city fled there, too; and those who lived in other cities; and those who lived in the villages, in the country, in the furthest regions.

15. Because his voice was heard all over the Island. And, at his call, children came out not only of the débris, but of the earth, too: from anywhere where man had cultivated the soil.

16. And thus all the inhabitants of the Island fled to the mountains, and hid themselves there. Because they believed that there they would be safe and remain undiscovered by the man who came from the sea.

17. Actually, in hiding from him, they were hiding from themselves.

18. And because of this, none of them felt safe. Because one cannot feel safe from that from which one imagines oneself to be hiding.

19. And it happened that a new earthquake, centred in the mountains, made all those who had been hiding there disappear into the sea amidst the roar of tumbling rocks.

20. Only two or three hundred escaped from the earthquake with their lives. And they lived to testify about the injustice in which they had participated, and which ended that day.

21. And from that day forth, the reign of the children began on the Island. Because the time for children to govern men had arrived. And the survivors were governed by them from that day forth.

22. And when they came down from the mountains and returned to the square, they found thousands of children there, and among them was the man in the white tunic. And, becoming luminous again, he returned to the sea.

23. And then a cloud in the shape of a circle descended to surround him, and, suffused with light, it quickly carried him up to the heavens where he disappeared.

An Appreciation

In a striking departure from his previous work, Herberto Sales has written a satire condemning the evils of a monolithic state backed by all the power of modern technology. Set in a futuristic world faced with the Malthusian spectre of starvation, the ruling technocrats are determined to put a stop to human procreation. Initial measures calling for mandatory abortion within the early months of gestation have failed to keep pace with the long lines of fecund females awaiting their turn. To meet the emergency all the machinery of the oligarchy is called into action. The Pill becomes law in the war against the womb for all women from adolescent to senescent. But Joseph, the carpenter, and his wife Mary (the allusion is obvious), have defied the authorities. Their child is born in a cave. The fugitives escape by boat and sail off into the unknown to bear witness to the world's iniquity. Thirty years later a Christ-like figure comes over the sea. The earth trembles and out of the ruins the children appear.

The message is clear, though it rings as true as a medieval morality play. There is neither the power nor the pessimism here of Anthony Burgess's chaotic world of *The Wanting Seed*, a world in which overpopulation is solved by cannibalism and wars without anger. What is refreshing about it is Sales' over-riding optimism, his supple style, gentle mockery, and compassionate treatment of the theme.

Structurally the book is divided into three parts, all of them dramatically different in tone and technique. However, these differences in no way detract from the cohesiveness of the work.

The first part is short and reads like a fairy tale. (Sales has published a number of children's books.) In a simple, ingenuous style, it tells the sad story of the rabbits whose fate it was to reproduce at so rapid a rate that eventually they became a threat to man and had to be exterminated.

This brief fable serves as a fictional analogue for the second or main part of the book which is an amusing mock-heroic episode ridiculing the technocrats at work. There are no characters, only faceless caricatures. They speak in elaborate syllogisms, skillfully contrived by the satirist who playfully parodies the tortuous dialectics of the masterminds of the world as they sit in emergency session, blindly plotting a course for human extinction. Indeed, at times it is positively dizzying to follow the convolutions of their distorted thinking. Here the voice of the *persona* has changed perceptibly from that of the *ingénu* clucking sympathetically over the 'poor little rabbits', to that of the malicious observer standing on the sidelines, diminunizing the authorities, at times through the eyes of an *alter ego* who sees them as 'mechanical dolls', at times *in propria persona*, darting in and out of the narrative with observations designed to make the reader rhetorically aware, by taking him into his confidence, in picaresque fashion, with a conspiratorial 'you and I'.

But the reader is in for a surprise in the third and final part of the book which is in sharp contrast to the rest. The impact is visual as well as literary since it is intended to resemble the Bible in form and content and is printed in reduced type and double columns, complete with chapter headings and verse numbers. The *persona* has now faded into the background, speaking in awed tone and biblical style as he chronicles the flight of Joseph and Mary and the birth of a saviour.

It is easy to share the author's indignation at the mindless despots of the world, though not as easy to share his mystic faith in the moral order of things. Nevertheless, it is a very readable book of timely and universal significance that should be made available in translation. Indeed, in a certain sense it is an event to be hailed, for it is not often that a Brazilian novelist ventures outside the confines of regionalism.

REBECCA CATZ

Santa Monica College

Reprinted from *The Modern Language Journal,* Vol. LXII, Nos. 5-6, September-October, 1978.

184 ABERYSTWYTH LIBRARY U.C.W. ★

Abbreviations

ASRA	Agricultural Services Recreational Apprenticeship
CARRIF	Council for the Application of Resources with Retroactive Investment of Funds
CCOSMOS	Council for the Co-ordination of Special Missions
CCRIP	Centre for Contraceptive Work to Improve the Pill
CENTRAF	Central Traffic
CLAN	Council on Legislation and Norms
CONSTAT	Contraceptive Strategy
CVP	Confidential Veto Power
DCs	Domestic Commandos
DECOWL	Department of Communications and Oral and Written Languages
DEPREGNACC	Department of Population Regulation and Nuptial and Collateral Counselling
DEVICOM	Department of Visual Communication
IVPO	Institute for the Verification of Public Opinion
KIT	Council of Integrated Technology
PAPA	Programme for the Assessment of the Population's Activities
SCAN	State Complex of Amalgamated News
SD	Subdeveloped
SICS	Situational Control Service
SPAIT	Services for Professional Adaptation with Intensive Training
SSOVPO	Sector for the Sampling of Public Opinions from the Verification of Public Opinion
SUPERCAP	Superior Consultants Planning Division
TechTAF	Technical Task Force
TECOPRICO	Technical Commission for Price Controls
TOPMIRE	Total Plan for Mass Information with Repetitive Extension
UNISEND	Unified Services for Newspaper Delivery